Coming Home

From

Gerry Sawyer 2002
(see dedication pages)

Coming Home

By Sheila Ryan Wallace

Enjoy the book! :)
Sheila Ryan Wallace

ISBN 0-7414-0956-9

Published by:

PUBLISHING.COM

519 West Lancaster Avenue
Haverford, PA 19041-1413
Info@buybooksontheweb.com
www.buybooksontheweb.com
Toll-free (877) BUY BOOK
Local Phone (610) 520-2500
Fax (610) 519-0261

Printed in the United States of America

Printed on Recycled Paper

Published April, 2002

Dedication

I dedicate this book, to God, my Creator, from whom I have received my love of language and storytelling. May He be glorified through all my writings.

Secondly, this book is dedicated with all my love to my husband, John Wallace, whose encouragement in all my endeavors has inspired, motivated, and challenged me to believe in myself. Thank you, John, for your steadfast patience, support and love, which enable me to explore my creativity.

To my children, Debbie, Cheryl, Bonnie, John, Scott, and Sharon, who often ask if my book is published yet. Thank you for your love and support. To those of the family who read my manuscript, thank you for your help with proof reading. To those of you who assisted me with understanding my computer so that I might more easily format my work, a big thanks.

To my parents, Earl E. Ryan, (deceased), and Vivian Gray Ryan, who throughout their lives have constantly supported me with their encouragement, love, and unwavering belief in my talents, thank you. Also, Mom, thank you for always being in my corner with your unflagging enthusiasm to read my latest work.

Acknowledgments

To my creative writing teacher, Nancy Mace, a thank you for the quickie class assignment that resulted in the seed for this book. To you and all the members of my Creative Writing Workshops, I extend my heartfelt thanks for the hours you've spent listening to my chapters and patiently critiquing each section. Many of your suggestions were very helpful.

To Bonnie Lee, for your work in the final editing, I am very grateful. To Gwen Austin, thanks for your prodding to get on with it and get it published.

To the members of the Tacoma Writers' Club, my appreciation for your support and for all that I have learned while attending our meetings.

To Zilpha McCarty, I appreciate your patient listening and helpful suggestions. To Patricia and Bill Smurro, and Gerry Sawyer, true friends who never stopped believing in me, thank you for your wonderful daily encouragement.

"This book shows cruelty can be passed down, change is possible, looks are deceiving, and trust can be earned and learned."

Bonnie Lee

Coming Home

Prologue

March, 1939

Stan stood over her, his booze-smelling breath creating a suffocating stench in the airless bedroom. Joy lay on her side, eyes closed, breathing evenly. She'd heard him come in and stumble around the kitchen. He'd been gone all evening, and she knew without a doubt that he was drunk. She pretended to be asleep knowing that if he even suspected she wasn't, there'd be hell to pay.

He stood there for what seemed like an eternity, then turned and staggered down the hall to the bathroom. She could hear him in there, muttering.

"Damn woman, you'd think she could stay awake and greet her man when he comes home." He flushed the toilet and she heard him bump the wall as he headed back to their room. A few minutes later he fell into bed beside her. He reached out and yanked her to him and she smothered a cry as he wrenched her arm. "S'matter? Can't you come over here by me?" he growled, "without moanin'?"

He began rubbing his hands roughly over her back, then grabbed her nipples. She steeled herself to go on pretending she was asleep. Stan was so far gone that he lacked the energy to pursue his amorous advances. He passed out with his hand on her breast.

She remembered a time when she'd welcomed his caresses. Stan had seemed so worldly, always joking, telling her outrageous stories of his 'experiences' with other women. She knew he was making most of them up, because she had been his sweetheart in high school, and she knew he hadn't had time to do all these things he was tellin' her. Still, it made him feel good to pretend he was a stud, and it aroused her to listen to him, 'specially when his hands was all over her. It was what had attracted her to him in the first place, this air of sophistication he put on.

Then Katie'd come along, and Stan kept wantin' to go on partyin'. When she'd just wanted to stay home with her baby. At nineteen, he was too young to be a father, she thought, and was afraid of the responsibility. He'd takin' to stayin' out late with his buddies, comin' home sloppy drunk and soon was takin' out his frustrations on her. Now, she could barely stand to have him touch her.

After lying there ten minutes scarcely daring to breathe for fear he'd wake, she finally slid out from under his arm and crept out of bed. One more time she'd avoided intimacy with him. She knew it wouldn't last, and that he'd use her again whenever he pleased. She quickly went to the bathroom, then looked in on Katie who was sleeping in the little storeroom at the end of the hall. Satisfied that her little one was peaceful for the time being, Joy made herself a cup of tea. She sat down at the kitchen table and wrote a note to her mother.

Ma,
Katie's asleep and I'm havin a cup of tea. I remember when you and me would stay downstairs after Pa would pass out, and we'd drink our tea together. It was a special time an' I always felt comfort from it. I'm gonna teach Katie to have that comfort, too.

She sat there awhile after she finished her note and thought of her Ma. Joy missed her company. It had been over four years since she'd seen her. She'd tried to get Stan to return home to Enterprise when he'd lost his last job, but he refused to even think about it. They'd burned their bridges as far as he was concerned, and he wasn't about to go back to the town where he was raised, letting folks know he needed a handout.

Instead, they'd muddled along with the little she'd been able to earn in her part-time job, till he'd found work at the gravel pit. This had brought in a small but regular paycheck, but Stan had given her very little of it. Most of it was squandered on booze and card games.

Finished with her tea, she silently crawled into bed, pulling herself over to the far wall. She lay there scrunched into a tight ball until she was sure he wasn't going to waken, then at last she let herself relax and sink into a fitful sleep.

"Momma. Momma," Katie called from her bed. Joy struggled to rise from the deep slumber she'd finally fallen into about daybreak. "I'm hungry, Momma," the child called from her bedroom.

Joy moved out from under the leg Stan had flung over her in his sleep. Shivering in the cold house, she pulled her worn robe tightly around her and trudged down the hall. "Hush, Katie. Don't wake your Daddy." She stretched, smothered a yawn and held out her arms to her daughter. "Come here, Punkin, and give your Momma a hug." She held Katie close and buried her head in the sweet, soft hair, knowing she'd do anything for this child. "Now let's go get our breakfast," she said.

She fixed a batch of oatmeal, which they ate silently, then dressed Katie and the two of them left the house. They walked four blocks in the biting cold to her housecleaning job at the home of Dr. and Mrs. Mullen. Katie looked forward to their days there for the house was always warm, and she liked to play with their two-year-old daughter.

Mrs. Mullen greeted them warmly. "Hello, Joy. Hi, Katie. Alicia's been waiting for you. She's in the playroom. Come on in out of the wind, both of you. I can't believe we have such a wintry cold this first day of Spring."

Stan woke about noon. "Dammit! I overslept again. Well, I don't feel like workin' in that G.D. gravel pit today anyways. I'll just tell 'em I was sick." He scowled as he thought of the last conversation he'd had with his boss, Ron, when Stan had missed work on another Monday morning after a two-day bender. Ron had threatened to dock his pay for not showing up and to fire him if he missed more than three days between now and summer. "Where does he get off threatenin' to fire me if I miss again?" he muttered to himself. "There ain't no justice. Can't even show no carin' or understandin' when a man's sick."

He filled a bowl with oatmeal from the pot on the stove. Still mumbling about the injustices of the world, he took one bite, then heaved the spoon across the room. "Damn it all. Oatmeal's cold and stiff. Think Joy'd know how to leave a man a decent breakfast."

The hell with it, he thought. He'd treat himself to a MAN'S breakfast at the diner. Yanking his jacket off the hook he went out, slamming the door behind him. Damn, it was cold. He buttoned up quickly, and shoved his hands in his pockets, setting off at a brisk walk. Mike's Place was situated one street off Main, about six blocks away. Hoping for a ride, he stuck his thumb in the air whenever he heard a car approach.

Sure was glad he'd found this winter jacket at Grant's right after Christmas. He'd gone in there to get out of the cold, and it was sitting right there in a clearance bin for one quarter of its original price. It was missing a button, but he'd found it in a pocket. When he'd got home from his card game, he'd wakened Joy at 2:00 a.m. and made her sew it on right away before it got lost.

Then he'd forced her into submitting to his rough love-makin'. She'd begged him to stop he was so drunk. Katie had had her up three nights runnin' with a fever and Joy herself had caught a helluva cold. She whined about being tired and sick, but he couldn't help it if his body craved some attention. Anyways, that's what women were for, his Pappy'd always said. So he wasn't takin' anything that didn't rightfully belong to him. He grinned to himself, liking the feeling of power he got when he thought of orderin' Joy to do what he wanted.

He buttoned the top button and hunched into the wind. *This G.D. gravel pit job*, he thought. He'd be glad when he could tell them they could take it and shove it. All it would take was for him to get lucky one of these nights at cards. Then he'd tell Joy she could shove it, too, and he'd walk. Oh yes, he'd walk. And he wouldn't give her or the brat a backward glance. Come to think of it, maybe he wouldn't wait to get lucky at cards. Maybe he'd walk one of these days anyways.

His fingers were half frozen when he strutted into Mike's Place and he blew on them to warm them up. He tossed a smile in the waitress's direction and took over a booth in a corner back by the restrooms. "Bring me a #1 and a mug of coffee on the double, Darcy, and come on back here. It's time for your break."

The waitress ran her tongue over her lips and fluffed up her blonde locks. Glancing at her few customers, she spoke to Herbie, the waiter. "Bring a #1 to Stan, will ya, Herbie? And take over for me? I'm gonna take my break now." She poured two mugs of coffee and slipped into the booth across from Stan. "Where ya been, honey? Ain't seen ya in three days."

Chapter One

August, 1939

The town of Enterprise choked in the late August dust. Storm clouds over the horizon had been building throughout the long, sweltering day.

Blanche sank down on the rickety front porch and fanned herself listlessly with the newspaper. She stared across their small family farm beyond the endless bare fields and tinder dry hills toward town.

Joe hitched up his suspenders, stretched, yawned, and plopped down on the worn davenport. "Why're ya starin' down the road? Ain't gonna get her home no faster. Just a couple more mouths to feed, anyways." He turned over and closed his eyes, hoping to catch a nap before their wayward daughter returned, bringing their first grandchild.

Blanche ignored him, and continued to search the far away hills for the second-hand jalopy that would bring her a reason to enjoy life again. After awhile she reached into her apron pocket and slipped out the crinkled letter she'd carried with her ever since it arrived in the mail two weeks ago. She laid it on her lap and nervously ran her hands over and over it trying to smooth the creases. Tiredly she picked it up and held it arm's length from her body, reading the words she knew by heart.

Dear ma,

I need your help. I'm comin back cause I ain't got no wheres else to go. Stanley run off, and Katie and me are hungry. Besides I don't know nuthin bout raisin kids.

Tell pa he don't have to worry none bout havin to support us. I'll find work and earn my keep. I'm drivin a '32 roadster.

We'll be there the fifteenth, some time in the afternoon if the jalop don't give out.

Joy

Blanche sat thinking about her runaway daughter. At 15 years of age Joy had taken to wearing tight sweaters, proud of the womanly figure she had developed. Joe yelled at her, calling her a tramp, every time he saw her dressed up to go out or standing in front of the bathroom mirror. Things came to a head one day, when Joy returned home early from a dance, crying because a boy had made a pass at her.

Joe exploded when he overheard her telling her mother. He'd been drinking beer steadily that evening trying to forget his worries about paying the bills. When he heard Joy say her date had been feeling her breasts, he threw the beer bottle against the wall. Grabbing her by the hair he yanked her into her bedroom.

"Slut!" he yelled, "What did he do to you?"

"N'nuthin, Pa! I w…wouldn' let him," Joy sobbed, cowering against the wall.

"I don' b'lieve you, missy. Always primpin' 'n carryin' on. You've jus' been askin' for it," he shouted wildly, slapping her across the face so hard he left the imprint of his hand on her cheek. Joy's head snapped back against the wall, and she felt something crack around her neck causing a sharp sting in her shoulder. She slumped to the floor screaming with pain. Blanche ran in and shouted at Joe to get out and leave Joy alone.

Surprised at the violence within that had unleashed like a demon out of control, Joe's fight left him and he backed out of the room. Blanche helped Joy undress and put her to bed. She placed a cold cloth on her face and soothed her daughter as best she could. When Joy at last sobbed herself to sleep, Blanche went to the kitchen to have it out with Joe.

"That's the last time you'll hit her or me either," she yelled, her anger at last giving her the courage to face this man who'd knocked all the fight out of her, whenever he'd lashed out in anger and frustration in the past. "I'll cook an' clean cause I'm married to you for better or worse, but this is the last day you'll touch me or Joy," she bristled, hardly able to contain her fury. "If you do, we're both out of here and you'll never see either of us again."

Joe stared at her. Blanche's eyes blazed with the intensity of a lightning storm. He'd never seen the quiet woman he'd married like this, in all the years he'd known her, and he knew she meant everything she said.

"Aw Blanche, you know I didn't mean to hit her that hard. I just want her to know she can't fool around, that's all." He walked over to his wife, and tried to put his arm around her.

Wham! Joe found himself on the floor before he knew she'd raised her arm to swing at him.

"I told you you're not goin' to touch me ever again," Blanche said. She pulled out a ragged blanket from the chest of drawers, and tossed it at him. "You can sleep on the couch from here on out."

After that things were more peaceful, but the little house was silent. Joe continued drinking, yet somehow managed to keep better control of his temper. Like all bullies he slunk away from those who weren't afraid to stand up to him. He and

Blanche endured a truce of sorts, and he avoided any major confrontations with her. They exchanged few words, just enough to get the chores done.

Joy's heart hardened toward her father, and she refused to speak to him at all. Finally, one day she ran away. She wrote a short note to her mother saying she was tired of never having any fun, and she was going to marry a boy she'd met at a dance. Now she was twenty and coming home with a four-year old child and no husband.

It grew noticeably darker, the air growing more and more oppressive. Nothing moved but the roiling black clouds assembling far above them. Low distant rumbles became gradually more frequent, increasing in volume as the storm neared. Restlessly Blanche stood up and descended the steps to the yard. She paced back and forth between house and barn, stopping only to calm the horses and the cow, who huddled together pawing the ground nervously with each rumble.

She was walking toward the barn when a sudden gust of wind nearly knocked her off her feet. Squinting her eyes against the blowing dust, she stared in horror at the funnel cloud that appeared on the horizon. The wind began to swirl the dust, which stung her bare arms as she quickly herded the animals into the pasture.

"Twister!" she yelled to Joe, still sacked out on the porch sofa. Her words were torn away by the wind, and she knew he couldn't hear her. She tried to hurry to the porch to tell him as the gusts tore at her skirt, wrapping it around her legs and impeding her progress. She dropped to the ground where the wind wasn't quite as strong, and crawled on her knees to the steps.

"Joe!" she shouted. "There's a tornado coming! Hurry!"

Joe sat up, still groggy from his nap. "Wha...what?" He mumbled.

Blanche had at last gained the top of the porch. "Hurry," she yelled again pulling him from the couch. "We've got to get to the storm cellar."

The two of them stumbled across the clearing in the general direction of the nearby shelter, holding on to each other for support from the wind. Dust spun around them so thick that they were unable to fully open their eyes to see where they were going. Choking from the dirt they held their shirts up over their faces, making slow progress toward the shelter. At last they reached it and Joe held the heavy door open while Blanche half fell, half slid down the steps to safety.

Joe quickly latched the door, nearly falling down the steps himself in his haste to get out of the weather. Finding matches where he had placed them in a moisture-proof box, he lit the oil lamp, and they sat huddled in the dim light to wait out the storm.

"Joe, what about Joy and the baby?" Blanche screamed when she'd caught her breath from their hazardous flight. She jumped up and started for the trap door above them. "I've got to find them!"

Joe grabbed her legs, slowing her climb. "Hold it, Blanche. You can't get 'em in this storm."

"Let me go! They're out there all alone," she sobbed, but Joe held on tight.

"Don't be foolish, woman. You're not goin' nowhere. In case you didn't notice that's one hell of a storm out there." He pushed her back against the wall, his roughness effectively masking his concern. For despite their enmity, he knew she was the glue that held him together, and he didn't want to lose her. "All we need's for you to get picked up by that twister. You won't be any help to 'em then."

Blanche pulled away from him as far as she could in the cramped space. She glared at him in the semi-dark until finally she realized he couldn't see her clearly enough to know it.

Closing her eyes she sat without speaking, her thoughts drifting to her daughter and the unknown granddaughter, Katie. It was over four years since 16-year old Joy had left, taking all of Blanche's joy with her. Joe and Blanche had plodded along, working to put food on the table, but the days dragged on endlessly the same. The only break in the monotony was when one of Joy's infrequent notes came.

Because Blanche blamed Joe for driving Joy away, she barely tolerated living with him. They had returned to sleeping in the same bed, but had not resumed any kind of sex life. One exception was when Joe drank himself into a half stupor and climbed onto her in the middle of the night. Blanche was half-asleep and dreaming, so gave in to his demands, needing the release as much as he. They never spoke of it and in the morning it was as though it had never happened.

Now she remembered that night and how good it had felt, despite the long enmity between them. It had reawakened passions within her that were common place in the first years of their marriage, passions she had all but forgotten. Since Joy's leave taking, it was as if a stranger shared her bed. She shifted position, and inadvertently brushed against Joe's arm with her breast. Joe sat up straighter. "Blanche?" he murmured.

"What?"

"I was thinkin'."

"What?" She rubbed her back against the wall impatiently.

"I...oh nuthin'." He lapsed into silence. They could hear the crashing of storm debris above them. Blanche tried to pray for Joy and Katie, but she had given up on praying a long time ago, and couldn't think how to begin. She wondered where they were and if they were safe. She hoped that Joy had had the sense to get off the highway and find a shelter till the storm passed. "Blanche?" Joe spoke once again.

"What?"

"Are you all right?"

"Yeah." Blanche shifted position again, wondering why Joe asked her that. He so seldom spoke it was a surprise to hear him. His voice had sounded concerned about her, but she knew better. With the exception of that one night, they'd not exchanged an affectionate word or embrace in over three years. It would be a hot day at the North Pole if he were to show her any concern, she thought. She squirmed again as the noise overhead became louder. It sounded as if a freight train were going by, and Blanche curled up in a ball and whimpered.

Suddenly the door to the shelter flew open, and Joe disappeared up the stairwell. Blanche screamed as she felt herself being sucked up right behind him. She held on to the concrete foundation, and realized Joe's legs were just above her. He was holding on to the heavy door, as the wind twisted around them. Her fingers were numb, and she began to lose her grip.

Chapter Two

The wind pried Blanche's hands loose and suddenly she felt herself dropping backwards down the stairs. She shrieked when she felt a sharp pain in her ankle. Joe rolled down the steps, coming to a stop on top of her, and she yelped again.

"What is it, Blanche?"

"My ankle!"

"Let's see." He lifted her foot and felt for a break. "Don't seem broken, but it's swelling; prob'ly have to stay off it awhile." He lowered her foot and stood up. "I think that twister's gone on by. Stay here till I check." Again Blanche saw him disappear up the steps. In too much pain to argue, she slumped back against the wall and shut her eyes.

How'm I to stay off my feet with all the chores to do, she wondered. *There's cookin' an cleanin' and animals to feed.* She became aware of the heavy pounding of rain on the trapdoor above, and realized she'd become soaked through when the tornado had grabbed her. Shivering, she thought of her daughter, fearing for her safety. She felt the rain once more as the door above her was raised.

"Blanche, you can come up now." Joe's face appeared above her.

She stood up, but as soon as she put weight on her injured foot, she cried out in pain and crumpled back down to the floor. "I can't," she whispered, fighting back tears. Joe descended the stairs and sat beside her.

"Lean on me," he said. "See if you can hop on your good foot." Blanche once again tried to stand, but her ankle ached with the effort.

"Let me go up on my knees," she said, and began to slowly crawl up the steps, Joe behind her trying to protect her foot. When they reached firm ground, she found a sturdy tree limb, which had blown down in the storm. Using it as a crutch, she hopped across the now muddy yard to the house. Once there, she sat on the steps and gazed around at the storm damage.

Half of the barn was gone. The cow mooed plaintively in the far corner of the pasture and the horses had gotten loose and were standing by the chicken house pawing the ground. The giant oak in the front yard was split in two and she could see the farm wagon upside down across the road.

"Where's the tractor?" she asked, as she looked at the empty space near the barn where it had been parked.

Joe looked up and scowled. "I dunno! I'll look for it later. Let's get inside and dry off." He opened the front door. "I'm sure it ain't going nowhere from where it's at, not unless another twister comes along."

Blanche shuddered as she thought of the destructive power that had just passed. She stood up with the help of the tree limb and hobbled into the house. "I'll make us some tea," she said and headed for the stove.

"Get off that foot," Joe said, taking the kettle from her. "I'll get the tea." She sank down on a kitchen chair, while Joe pulled over another for her foot to rest on. He found a pillow and placed it on the chair, then gently lifted her leg. When she was settled, he took a tray of ice out of the refrigerator and shook it loose into the sink. Wrapping a few ice cubes in a dishtowel, he laid them on her ankle.

Blanche felt awkward watching Joe bustle around her kitchen. She couldn't remember the last time he'd helped in the house. There was always too much to do outside. They had talked so little since Joy had left that she couldn't think of anything to say to him now.

Joe glanced at her. "I'll go out and see if we still have any chickens, while that water's heatin'." He left the house, and Blanche sat worrying about Joy and Katie.

Joe approached the chicken house, where he could hear a squawking going on. The chickens luckily were all there, but were complaining loudly at the shovel that stood like a tree right in the middle of the hen house. Its handle was imbedded too deep to pull out by hand, and it had pierced a hole in the roof. The shovel end stuck up above the roof like an iron flag. Joe searched for eggs, and was surprised to find three that were still whole. "Thanks for supper," he told the clucking birds, as he gingerly carried the eggs back to the house.

"Blanche?" He stepped into the kitchen. "Chickens are fine, got some eggs."

"We'll have scrambled eggs and toast for supper then," Blanche said.

She started to get up to fix their meal, but Joe said, "Sit down, Blanche, I'll fix it. I think I can still remember how to scramble an egg."

Blanche was surprised to see Joe being so helpful. She remembered when they were first married he'd liked to help her in the kitchen, but it had been years. What had happened to them?

She sighed, thinking of how they'd drifted apart with Joe's increased drinking and the meanness it had brought on him. "Foot hurtin'?" Joe asked.

"No."

They ate in silence, both having run out of words.

Joy glanced at the gas gauge. The needle hovered just above empty. Driving down the winding country road, she spotted a farmhouse that she recognized, and breathed easier knowing that the gas would hold out till she got home.

"Momma, I gotta potty." Four-year old Katie squirmed beside her.

Joy pulled over to the side of the road. She stood beside the car and wiped the perspiration from her face while Katie squatted behind a bush. The air felt dense and thick, seeming to press in on her. She looked around at the bleak countryside. Now that the noise of the car engine had ceased, she became aware of the absolute quiet of the surrounding terrain. Not a blade of grass moved and usually chittering birds were silent. She heard the faint rumble of distant thunder, and off on the horizon spotted some dark thunderheads.

"Hurry, Katie. We gotta get there 'fore it storms."

Katie pulled up her panties and returned to the car. They resumed their journey, Joy now anxiously trying to out race the storm, and becoming increasingly nervous over her impending reunion with her parents. Clouds overhead became dark green and wild looking. She could see them twisting and churning like stew in a boiling kettle of water.

Uneasily she felt the thickness of the air and realized she was breathing in short, struggling breaths. Katie was now unusually quiet. She glanced at the normally chattering child beside her and saw that she was looking wide-eyed and fearful. Returning her eyes to the road, Joy hit the brakes in shock as she saw the huge funnel cloud that had suddenly formed in the distance. Looking wildly around for shelter, she spied a low-lying wooden bridge over a small creek on a farm property. The farmhouse itself sat on a hill a distance from the road. Knowing there wasn't time to reach it Joy hollered, "Hurry, Katie!"

Grabbing the child's hand she pulled her out of the car, and they scrambled down the incline to shelter under the bridge. They had barely reached it when the clouds seemed to open up, pouring down hail the size of marbles. The din on the bridge overhead sounded like the rat-a-tat-tat of bullets from a gun Joy had once heard at the County Fair. Keeping their feet out of the stagnant water, they huddled on the grassy bank against the pilings.

"Momma, Momma!" Katie screamed in fright, as the wind suddenly blew her hair across her face obstructing her vision. Joy pulled the child against her. "Momma, I'm skeered. I wanna get in the car."

"Shhh, we're just goin' to hide here till the storm goes on by." The wind picked up strength, and Joy, shaking in fear, folded herself over her daughter.

The silence became a deafening roar as if all the animals in the world were growling their displeasure. They heard a crack as a tree was uprooted, but both were so frightened they lay with their eyes shut.

Joy held on to the under-post of the little bridge as the wind tried to sweep them loose. Katie, too terrified to cry, whimpered once then lay still, clinging to her mother. The noise increased in volume. Still they kept their eyes tightly shut. There was a sound of metal hitting pavement. Storm debris whirled around them, fence posts and tree limbs flying through the air like bullets.

At last the twister moved on and silence reigned once more. Trembling, Joy raised her head and looked down at her frightened child. "Katie, are you all right?"

"Momma, I wanna go home," the child sobbed, rubbing her tear-streaked face against her mother's breast.

Joy pulled her daughter close and crooned to her. "We're goin' home, baby, we're going home. Let's go now." She scrambled up the embankment, tugging Katie by the hand. Reaching the road they looked around in bewilderment.

"Momma, where's our car?"

"I don't know, honey. I left it right here," Joy responded in confusion. "Oh, no!" she moaned. She stared up the road at her vehicle and began to run toward it, Katie at her heels.

"It's upside down, Momma. How can we drive it?" the little girl asked.

"I don't know, Katie." Joy closed her eyes, said a quick prayer, and began to look around for help, as both of them became aware of the persistent rain and the drop in temperature.

"Momma," Katie wailed, "I'm cold."

"Look," Joy said. "A farmhouse. Up on that hill. Let's go see if someone can help us." By the time they reached the farmhouse half a mile away, both were shivering so hard their teeth chattered uncontrollably.

The house was surrounded on three sides with a wrap-around porch. Tall poplars stood close together along one side of the dwelling and across the back yard, forming a windbreak. Two giant oak trees spread their protective covering close to the house on the other side, while a lone apple tree stood guard in the front yard. Gusting winds had knocked a couple of tree limbs down on to the side porch, damaging the porch roof and rail, but the rest of the house and outbuildings seemed intact. Joy and Katie stepped carefully around the fallen branches and knocked at the door.

A tall man swung it open and stared down at them. Joy stepped back, intimidated by a bushy beard and a tangled mass of wavy brown hair badly in need of a trim. "C-can you help us? A t-twister t-turned our c-car over and we c-can't g-get home," she stuttered, unable to keep her chattering teeth under control. The man looked at the bedraggled pair before him, taking note of the petite woman's full breasts as her soaked dress clung to her body.

"Oh, say you'll help us, mister." The child looked up with huge dark eyes fixed directly on his. She didn't waver even as he looked sternly down upon her from his great height. The man's lips softened a bit as he hid the smile triggered by the child's earnestness.

"Wal, come on in. We'll see what we can do, little one." He turned back into the house, Joy and Katie trotting cautiously after him.

They were in a square shaped kitchen of moderate size. The counters were cluttered with the makings of the evening meal, and their stomachs grumbled when they smelled cornbread baking in the oven. A pot-bellied stove stood in the corner, and the man threw some kindling in and started a fire, even though the house was comfortably warm.

"Come and get dry by the fire. I'll go have a look at your car." He pulled a rain slicker from a hook by the back door. Thrusting his arms into the sleeves he quickly left the kitchen and hiked out toward the road.

"Momma, I'm hungry." Katie rubbed her tummy, wanting desperately to taste the bread that gave off that heavenly smell. Joy sat down on an old wooden rocker by the fire and pulled Katie on to her lap. She slowly rocked back and forth.

"I know you are, Katie, but that's not our food. Hush now. When we get to Grammy's maybe she'll give us something to eat."

It wasn't long before the man returned. As he passed the kitchen window, he saw the young mother rocking her child by his fire, and stopped for a moment to watch. Nostalgic feelings stirred up by the sight brought back memories of the woman he'd married, killed when her car was run over by a train two years ago. A single tear rolled down his cheek, and he wiped it away angrily and marched in to the house.

"You're not going anywhere in that car tonight," he told Joy. "It'll take more than just me to turn it right side up. Then it'll have to be checked out to make sure it'll run okay."

Joy stared at him. "Well, I guess we gotta walk," she said, and stood up, setting Katie down on the floor.

The child immediately set up a wail. "Momma, I cain't walk. I'm too hungry! I want supper!" She plunked herself down in front of the fire and howled in anguish.

Chapter Three

The man winced as the shrieks became louder in volume and higher in pitch. "When's the last time you two ate?" he asked Joy.

"We had a piece of cheese about lunch time," she mumbled, shamed that she hadn't been able to give her child more.

"Wal, you can't go anywhere 'til that child has some vittels in her. I fixed some beans and cornbread. You can eat some if you want. What's yer little gal's name?"

"Katie."

"Wal, Katie might not want to eat beans, but there's some chicken soup in the icebox. I'll heat it up for her, and she can have some cornbread with it."

"Thanks, Mister. We'll pay you back soon's we can." Joy was too hungry to refuse.

"Name's Jake. You don't need to worry 'bout payin' me back. There's plenty, and if you don't eat it, it'd just go to waste." He set out some plates and forks, and reached up in the cupboard for some mugs. Within minutes the three were sitting at the round kitchen table, eating the tastiest supper Joy could remember having in a long time. Their host poured cold milk into Katie's mug, and hot coffee into Joy's and his own. They ate silently, the adults both a bit self-conscious and the child too hungry to speak. At last, their hunger satisfied, Jake sat back in satisfaction. "How far ya goin?" he asked Joy.

"To the Russell's place," she replied. "It's …".

"I know where it is," he interrupted her. "A good six miles down the road. You can't take that girl there tonight. She's asleep on her feet now."

Joy glanced at Katie who sat rubbing her eyes, struggling to stay awake. "I've gotta keep goin'. We don't have nowhere else to stay. My Ma will fix her a bed when we get there."

Just then Katie gave up the fight and slumped down in her chair fast asleep, her tummy full of hot soup and cold milk. Jake rose and quickly scooped the little girl up in his arms. He carried her to his spare bedroom and gently laid her on the bed. "You can sleep here tonight. There's another bed down the hall. In the morning we'll see if we can get your car back on the road." He grabbed a couple of blankets from a chest in the hall, and headed for the kitchen door.

"Where're you going?" Joy asked.

"I'll sleep in the barn. You don't have to worry about me. Lock the kitchen door if it'll make you feel better."

"Wait, we can't...." But he was gone. Joy looked around her in dismay. How could she take this stranger's house, and what's more his bed? But he did offer, and he was gone, and she was just too tired to chase him down and argue. Besides, her little girl was worn out.

With this last rationalization she realized she too was exhausted. She quickly locked the door, and lay fully dressed on Jake's bed. Almost immediately she fell sound asleep. Sometime in the night she awoke and took off her dress. Pulling the covers over her, she fell back asleep clad in her thin cotton slip.

Jake bedded down in the hayloft. Between the hay sticking in him every time he shifted position, and his thoughts of the woman in her drenched dress, he didn't get much sleep. Up early, he returned to the house to fix breakfast. Unlocking the door with the aid of a screwdriver, he quickly went to work in the kitchen.

When coffee was made, he scrambled some eggs and fixed buttered toast, then headed for the bedroom to call Joy. She lay sprawled across the bed in her slip, her covers thrown off. Jake, aroused by the sight, paused in the doorway. He stared at her for a long moment, then caught himself and backed away. He decided to wake the child first, and send her to awaken her mother. "Katie, come get some breakfast."

The child jumped up as soon as she heard his voice. "Wha...? Oh. Where's my Momma?"

"She's in the next room. Why don't you go wake her, then come get some eggs."

"Momma, Momma, we get to eat breakfast," Katie hollered as she ran into Joy's room. Jake frowned as he realized they must have been hungry for more than just their trip yesterday. He returned to the kitchen to make more toast.

During breakfast, Joy told him she was returning to live with her parents. Jake watched the curve of her breasts as they rose and fell with every breath she took. She'd put her hair up in a ponytail this morning, and he knew he'd seen her before. There was something about her that seemed very familiar.

"What did you do before you went away?" he asked her.

"I was in school."

"Dade School?"

"Yes."

"Did you work in the diner on weekends and wear your hair in a ponytail?"

"Yeah, how did you know?"

"How long you been away?" he asked.

"A little more'n four years."

"Well, that explains it.'

"What?"

"Why I didn't recognize you. I used to see you at that diner once in awhile, then I went away. I got back from my two years hitch in the army about three and a half years ago. Guess you must have just left."

"Yeah."

He pushed back his chair. "You can wait here, while I see about gettin' some help for that car."

"Where are you going for help?"

"There's a neighbor about a mile over that hill," he said, indicating a hill outside the window to the rear of the house. "I'll walk over there and fetch him. With luck, we'll have you on the road by this time tomorrow."

"Tomorrow! Oh no. Mister, I told you we have to git on home." Joy rose quickly. "C'mon, Katie. We're goin'. Much obliged, Mister." She grabbed Katie by the hand and went out the door.

Jake followed, shouting at her to come back. "Don't be crazy. It's going to get too hot," he hollered as she quickly walked across his yard toward the road. He ran after her and grabbed her arm. "Wait'll I hitch up the horses. If you're set on goin' I'll give you a ride."

But Joy was adamant, feeling she was already too much in his debt. She shook him off, and tugging Katie's arm, said: "We'll make it. C'mon, Katie girl."

"I wanna stay here, Momma. I want him to be my Daddy." Katie cried. "He's got food, and he's nice to me."

"Hush!'" Joy walked faster pulling Katie along, determined not to be obligated for anything more to the stranger. She knew she'd never have the means to pay him back.

"Wal, I'll be." Jake scratched his head in frustration at the willful woman walking down the road. He turned and went back to the house. When the dishes were done, and he'd seen to his farm chores, he hitched his two workhorses to the wagon, and set off to save the girl from her own folly.

Joy trudged along, Katie dragging behind her. They couldn't be half way there yet, and already the hot sun was making her feel weak. She wouldn't be in this mess if Stan had been the kind of man she'd thought he was, when she'd run off with him. How could she have been such a fool?

She remembered when they'd met. Stan had been so perky, always playin' little tricks on her to make her laugh. He seemed to like to make people happy in them days. But once he'd got her to hisself he'd changed. He'd take his temper out on her. Course he was always sorry after, and then he treated her real nice. But it never lasted very long.

Well, she'd made her bed, but she wasn't goin' to lie in it. He was gone now, and she'd never go back with him even if he came crawlin' back. She brushed her thick brown hair from her face and concentrated on putting one foot in front of the other.

Jake caught up to Joy about two miles down the road. She was plodding along, lifting her dark hair off her collar and wiping the sweat from her neck.

Katie trudged along behind her, kicking rocks as she went. Road dust clung to their clothes, and perspiration trickled down their flushed faces.

They turned toward him at the sound of the horses. Jake's heart hardened at the sight of Katie's bright red face, and he spoke sternly to her mother. "What are you trying to do, woman? Don't you know it's too hot to be taking a child on a hike? Get on up here, and I'll take you to where you're goin'."

Joy felt too weak from the heat to argue. She climbed up on to the seat, while Jake picked up an unusually quiet and sunburned Katie and set her down beside her mother.

"Giddyap," he shouted to the horses, lightly slapping their backs with the reins, and they were off. None of them spoke for a few minutes.

"Thanks," Joy said finally, breaking the silence. "Ma will be worryin'."

"Is that why you were in such a goldern hurry?"

"Yeah, she was expectin' us yesterday, and maybe thinks we got swallered up by that twister."

"Wal, when she sees you and that young'un all red an dusty, she's gonna think maybe that twister got you anyways." He turned the wagon on to a small dirt road and came to a stop in the shade of a big cottonwood tree.

"What are you doing?" Joy asked.

"We'll stop here for a bit and you can cool off in that crick over there, maybe get some of the road dust off you and Katie before you scare your ma half to death."

"Yay! Can I get wet all over?" asked Katie.

"Just your face and arms and legs," Joy answered. "Keep your dress dry much as you can."

They trotted down to the creek, and gratefully splashed water on their faces and arms. Jake followed behind them with a jug of water he'd retrieved from under his seat and they each took a long drink. After Joy brushed the dust off their clothes, he led them to a log under the tree. "Let's sit here a bit 'til you get rested 'fore you see your ma. Katie's face is red as a beet and yours looks like them red birds in winter. You know the ones, can't think of their names. Oh, yeah, the cardinals."

They sat on the log in the shade, Joy grateful for a water bath and cool drink. Katie could not sit still long. She explored the area around them, hunting for treasures. Finally she asked. "Momma, can I get wet again?"

"I guess so. Take your dress off and you can go in with just your panties. They'll dry fast in this heat," Joy said. Katie went scampering down to the creek once more. Joy watched her from the relative coolness of the shaded log. "It's good to see her havin' fun for a change," she said.

Jake watched the little girl splashing happily. "What do you mean? Doesn't she have fun every day?"

"She hasn't had much fun lately." Joy scowled, remembering the shouting and Stan's quick temper. "Her Daddy would whip her if she made any noise when he was on one of his drinkin' binges." She looked up to see Jake's outraged glare.

"What kind of man would whip a little sprite like that?" He jumped to his feet and angrily heaved a hefty rock into the water. "Where's her Daddy now?"

"He's run off and left us," Joy said. "That's why we're goin' back home." She rose to her feet. "And that's all I'm goin' to say about it, Mister. I think it's time we got back on the road. C'mon, Katie."

"Forget Mister, the name's Jake." He looked at the prickly woman beside him, and wondered what other hurts she had suffered from her man.

"Okay, Jake. We've gotta get going."

"Whatever you say, ma'am. You know, you never did tell me your name."

"Momma's name is Joy, Mr. Jake," Katie said as she came running up from the creek, dripping water as she ran. "Momma, Momma, do we have to go?"

Joy's face softened and she smiled down at the little girl, whose skin glowed from the creek water. "Remember, baby, we're on our way to Grammy's. She may need our help after the storm."

She gave Katie's dress a shake to rid it of any accumulated dust, then slipped it over her head. Jake boosted the little girl up on to the wagon seat, while Joy scrambled up the other side, not waiting for his help.

Blanche hobbled around the kitchen fixing lunch. Her ankle throbbed, but Joe was out trying to rebuild the barn. He'd fixed her some bacon and eggs for breakfast before he left to round up a couple of neighbors to help. Now it was her turn, she figured. The men would be hungry, and despite her pain she would have to give them something to eat. She cut some of the ham she was saving for Joy and Katie, and made sandwiches. There was still some of last year's homemade applesauce. She took down a jar and set it on the table, then went to the door to call Joe.

"Blanche, I told you to stay off that foot," he grumped as he stepped in to the kitchen a few minutes later.

"Do you think sandwiches are going to make themselves?" she snapped. "You've got to feed your helpers. *They* must be plenty hungry by now."

"We *all* are," he retorted. "We'll eat this out by the barn." He lifted the plate of sandwiches, the applesauce and utensils, and headed out the door. Blanche knew he would get the men some water from the well to drink. She wondered how long before that old well would go dry. Yesterday's rain was not enough to replace all they'd lost due to drought.

Her thoughts continued to ramble. The air in her little kitchen was stifling. She decided to rest her ankle on the porch and hopped outside on her good foot. She sank back on to the cushion, the leg stretched out in front of her.

Where is Joy, she wondered. *She could be lying helpless in a ditch. Leave it to Joe to take care of the animals first before he goes huntin' for his daughter.* Weary from the effort of preparing lunch with her aching ankle, she closed her eyes, the heat adding to her drowsiness.

Blanche awoke to the sound of a horse's whinnie, and looked up to see the approaching wagon and three passengers. "Joe, Joe, we got company," she hollered, smoothing down her hair as she stood at the edge of the porch to meet them. She wondered who would come to visit during the middle of a workday.

Joe came out of the barn and joined her on the porch, grumbling. "How's a man to get anything done around here, with people gallivantin' around like they got nothin' better to do?"

The wagon rolled into the yard, and came to a stop near the chicken house. Jake hopped down and turned to lift Katie. Gently he set her on her feet. He held out his arm to Joy, who surprised him by taking it. She stepped down from the wagon with the grace of a queen. Thanking him for the ride, she turned toward the porch.

Head held high she walked up the path and spoke. "I'm here, Ma. Pa, this here's your grandkid. Katie, say hello to your Grammy and Grampa."

Chapter Four

"H'lo," Katie mumbled, suddenly shy as she glanced up at the stern looking couple squinting down at her in the bright sunlight.

"You are welcome here, Joy." Blanche spoke stiffly, not knowing how to show affection to the young woman who had replaced her teen-age daughter.

"So. You've decided to come back, have you?" Joe growled, after recovering from the surprise of seeing this mature person who called him Pa. "Well, you're just in time to help your mother out, her laid up with a sore ankle and all. Don't expect her to be waitin' on you and that young'un of yours." He descended the stairs to the yard. "Now, I've got to be gettin' back to work."

He brushed past Jake who was tending to his horses. "Who are you?"

"Yes, who's that with you, Joy?" Blanche asked.

"I'm Jake Jorgeson, folks. I farm the old Grant spread east of town. Joy needed a lift after that tornado tinkered with her car, and I happened to have the horses and wagon, so here we are."

"Well, come in and have a cup of tea," Blanche offered, at last remembering her manners.

"No thanks, Ma'am. I've got to be getting back. My house needs a bit of repair too, after that twister. And the quicker I get back, the quicker I can get Joy's car back on the road." He turned to Joy. "I'll be in touch with you just as soon as I know somethin' about your car. We'll arrange a way to get it to you."

"I'll be over for it myself tomorrow, Mister. You don't need to trouble yourself."

Jake sighed. "The name's Jake, and it's no trouble." Knowing by now how strong-willed she was, he warned her not to show up before four o'clock. "I'll need at least that much time to get her running again." He reached down and squeezed little Katie's hand. "See you, pardner," he grinned.

"Bye, Mr. Jake." Katie watched him swing himself up on to the wagon and turn the horses toward the road. She stared after him longingly, then turned to Joy. "Momma, why doesn't my Grampa like me?" Katie's small voice whispered at her mother's elbow.

Joy looked angrily toward the barn, watching Joe stomp back to work. "He just doesn't know you yet, Katie. Now let's go see Grammy."

She climbed the stairs to the porch. When she reached her mother, she could see how fatigued she was. "Ma, you better get off that foot. It looks swollen and red. What happened, anyways?"

"The twister got me. When it dropped me, I rolled down the steps of the storm cellar and landed on my ankle." Blanche wearily settled back on the couch. "Joy, there's ham and bread in there. Why don't you fix us sandwiches and lemonade? Come here little Katie. Let me have a look at you."

Joy headed for the kitchen while Katie and her grandmother got acquainted. Later, Joy and Blanche spent the afternoon on the porch, fanning themselves in the heat. They talked very little about the years they'd been apart, neither of them easy with each other after their long separation. Instead, they filled one another in on their experiences of yesterday's storm.

Meanwhile Katie amused herself with exploring the chicken house and yard. After awhile the heat became so intense the little girl curled up on the end of the davenport and fell asleep. Tired from making conversation after her long spell of living in silence with Joe, Blanche soon closed her eyes and fell asleep herself.

Joy wandered through the house at a loss for something to do. She couldn't unpack until she got her car back, as everything she owned was in the vehicle. And that darn sure wasn't much, she thought. She climbed the stairs to her old room, and saw that nothing was changed. The cracked mirror hung above the wash stand as always. She pulled open a dresser drawer and looked through the few skirts and blouses she'd left behind.

None of them would fit now, she knew. As she lifted each one she shook it out, thinking some of them might be cut down for Katie. The last shirt was rolled tightly in the corner of the drawer. She remembered wearing it one night when she'd sneaked out to meet Stan. As she lifted it up, a piece of paper dropped from the pocket and fluttered to the floor

Joy retrieved it, sat on the edge of the bed and stared at it. Suddenly she was transported back to that evening nearly five years ago by the river. She read the note Stan had given her, remembering how much she'd believed in his love.

Baby, You and me are going places. We're not gonna be stuck in a hick town like this. Meet me at the river, and we'll show everybody. We'll shake the dirt from this crummy town for good. Come with me, baby, and we'll go to the city and spend the rest of our lives havin us a good time.

Love ya,
Stan

She reflected on how needy she'd been for love. *Now I'm smarter. Men can't be trusted. I'll make my own way, me and Katie. No man is gonna tell me what to do, or beat me again. I'll stay here in Pa's house just 'til I get enough saved to get a little place of my own.*

Joe's helpers left about supper time, the barn walls back up, and the roof on. He washed up at the pump in the yard, and headed for the kitchen where the women had set out the supper. As he drew near the apple tree, he was startled to hear a small voice call: "Hi, Grampa!"

Looking around, he could see no one. Again he heard: "Hi, Grampa." This was followed by a soft giggle. Joe looked up and caught sight of Katie's small face peering down at him through the leaves.

"Come down out of there," he hollered. "B'fore you ruin the apples."

"Okay, Gramps," said the irrepressible Katie, revived from her afternoon nap. She jumped off the tree branch and landed beside him, kicking up dust as she hit the ground. Grinning, she said, "I like it here, Grampa."

"Hmmph," he said. "Well, you'd better get on in there for supper."

"Okay, Grampa. Race you!" And she was off, running for the house.

"Hmmph," Joe muttered to himself "The child's got no sense at all, runnin' in this heat."

All through dinner, Katie chattered about the chickens, the apple tree, the storm they'd come through, until finally her grandfather threw down his fork and yelled at Joy. "For Chrissake, can't a man have peace in his own house. If you don't throttle that girl, I will!" He took his plate, and went out on the porch to finish his supper by himself.

Katie stopped her chatter and looked wide-eyed at her mother, a tear slipping silently down her cheek.

"Why is Grampa so mean, Momma?"

"He's just not used to kids around, Katie," Blanche answered as Joy strode for the porch determined to have it out with her father. "Come on, Katie, you can help me with the dishes."

"Oh yay, can I do the washing?" The little girl ran for the sink, pulling a chair over to the counter.

"Let me see if I can find something for you to wear as an apron. Did you know your Momma used to like helping me with the dishes when she was no bigger than you? She stood on that chair right there by the sink."

"She did?" The child's eyes were round with wonder as she tried to imagine her Momma as a little girl just her size and standing on a chair. Blanche smiled, happy she had succeeded in distracting Katie from the argument already beginning on the porch.

Outside Joy lit into her father. "Pa, I don't want you yelling at Katie. She's had too much yelling in her life, and I don't want her growin' up fearful and hatin' it here like I did."

"Is that so?" Joe blustered. "Well, Missy. We was getting along just fine before you got here today. If you want to change your mind about stayin', there's the road."

She glared at her father, turned on her heel, and walked back into the house. *Why does he hate me so,* she wondered. *He knows I can't leave now, not with Katie to care for.*

"Ma, I'll help Katie finish up," she said as she saw Blanche trying to remove the dishes from the table. "You get off that ankle."

Blanche gratefully left Joy and Katie with the cleanup, and headed out to the porch to join Joe. "How can you take your meanness out on a little girl?" she asked him.

"Now don't you start on me," he said, as she sank down beside him on the davenport. "I'll not have my wife and daughter tellin' me how to run my house."

Blanche sighed. *How will we work this out? He still has all that anger in him from the past and it's twisted his thinkin' toward Joy. Now he's gonna take it out on Katie, too.*

They sat in silence for a bit, then Joe heaved himself up, and set out to complete his evening chores. When he disappeared inside the barn, Joy came out to the porch, and sat in the rocker.

"Where's Katie?" Blanche asked.

"I put her up to bed in my old room. She's had a lot of excitement for one day, and is pretty tired."

"She's a sweet one, that girl, Joy."

"Yeah." Joy stared off toward the road. "Don't know if this is the right place for her."

"What do you mean?" Blanche panicked, afraid Joy would leave again.

"Well, I can't be off workin' if I have to worry about him being mean to her."

Blanche sat up straighter. "Joy, don't you worry about him none. I'll see that she's well taken care off. He's <u>not</u> gonna scare her like he did you with his yellin'."

Later, as Joy lay wide-awake in her old bed, she heard her parents' raised voices from the stairwell. She sighed. *I'd forgotten just how unreasonable Pa can be. He's so wrapped up in his work he's forgotten how to play, if he ever did know. Doesn't he know kids like to talk and have fun? Course he sure didn't want me to have any fun, I guess.*

Downstairs Blanche reminded Joe that Joy was a young woman now, and as Katie's mother she would have the say in bringing her up.

"You made the child cry, Joe."

"She must be a weak sister if she can't take a little yellin'."

"Joe, will you never learn some folks are worn down more by yellin' than by most anything else?"

"Maybe I *shoulda* throttled her then, is that what you're sayin?"

Blanche took a deep breath and began again, determined to make her point and not be goaded into an argument. "Joe, listen to me. Things are going to change around here with a young'un in the house. Don't you remember when Joy was little?

You used to like her to sit on your lap of an evenin' and tell you about her day."

Joe took a swallow of the beer he'd been nursing. "You've got it all figured out, haven't you, Blanche?"

"I'm just trying to see can't we work this out. God knows I'm glad to have my daughter home after these past lonely years. And I want to keep her here. And that little one is a sweet one. Don't drive them away, Joe."

Joe took another swallow of beer and stood up. He walked to the edge of the porch and looked at the newly repaired barn. *What does she want from me,* he wondered. *Don't I work hard here to keep a roof over her head?* He knew he was a failure, that she wanted more than that. Thinking back, he remembered when he had courted her. Blanche used to smile a lot. Now he realized she hadn't smiled since Joy had left home. *Maybe even before that,* he thought. He turned back to his wife. "What do ya want me to do, Blanche?"

"I'm just askin' you not to yell at the girl. Joy plans to find work and I'll be takin' care of Katie. If you drive them away, I don't think I'll be able to go on livin' with you."

"Just keep her outta my way, then," he snarled.

Chapter Five

Mumbling to himself, Joe marched into the kitchen for another beer. *Don't think she can live with me, hmm? Well, it'll be a cold day in hell if she thinks I'm gonna sit back and watch her go. Anyhow, she ain't goin' nowhere. She ain't got no money, and she don't have anyone to go to.*

He took the beer out back to drink by the woodshed. "Too bad a man can't have peace in his own house," he muttered into the night air, not admitting even to himself how wrong he was, yelling at Katie this evening. He thought of the child's mother. *That Joy's always caused trouble in this house.* He remembered when she was conceived. Blanche and he had been on a hayride at the Bartlett's. It was a beautiful autumn night. When they'd got home, he rolled out a blanket on the floor by the fire. Blanche had thought it romantic. She'd told him it was just like in a movie she'd seen.

We was pretty happy then, over the baby's comin'. Then there was more and more work every year, until there was no time for fun and hayrides. A couple bad years an' we almost lost the farm. Had to work long and hard to pay off our debts. 'Course Blanche helped. Have to give her credit for that. Takin' that job in town at the grocery store. Even took little Joy with her to work. Maybe that's why I'm not comfortable around the kid, Katie. I didn't really spend a lot of time with Joy.

He knew it was more than that though. He hadn't spent more time with Joy or Blanche because he'd taken to drinking beer every weekend to relax after his long days in the fields. He even made his own brew, and it didn't take too many drinks to make him fighting mean. He'd often pass out on the couch after two or three.

It wasn't until that time he'd slapped Joy against the wall that he'd realized the beer was getting a hold of him. After that he'd cut back his drinking and even stopped making his own. The store bought kind was less powerful and with money tight he couldn't always afford it anyway.

Swallowing the last of his beer he returned to the house and the front porch, only to find that Blanche had gone up to bed. He turned off the kitchen light and trudged up the stairs.

* * *

Jake stared at the shapely ankles approaching the car, and quickly jerked his head up for a better look. "Ow!" He hollered as he cracked his head on the bumper. He squirmed out from under the car where he'd been checking the brakes and stood up, rubbing his temple with a greasy hand.

"Wal, h'lo, Miss Joy." He grinned at her, liking what he saw. Joy was dressed in the same clothes she'd worn yesterday but Jake didn't notice. He was much more interested in the trim figure under the dress and the shiny dark hair curling around her collar than he was in the clothing she wore.

"Hi," Joy said. She was hot from her long hike but was anxious to get her car back, so had walked about three or four miles in the heat of the late afternoon. She'd managed to cut some of the distance by short cutting through the fields. "How bad is the car?" She asked. "Will it run?"

"I was just fixin' to take it for a test drive," Jake answered, smiling. "Why don't you get in and we'll try her out, see how she does?" Joy nodded and climbed into the passenger side as Jake started the car. He headed up the road toward the creek where they had rested the preceding day. After a few minor jerks the car moved along smoothly till Joy thought it ran better than it had before the tornado.

Jake too was pleased. "She's running like a dream," he said in satisfaction.

"Yeah, thanks, Jake. What do I owe you?" Joy asked, wondering how she'd ever get the money to pay him.

Jake reached the creek road. He pulled over and parked.

"You just paid me," he grinned.

"How?"

"By getting my name right."

Joy looked away, embarrassed. "I knew your name. I was just tired and worried."

"You don't have to apologize none. I reckon you had good reason to be."

"Yeah."

Removing his lanky body from the car, he flopped on the ground, head and back supported by a log. "Let's sit a spell," he said, beckoning her with a lazy smile. She got out of the car. When he closed his eyes Joy sat stiffly on the log watching him. He looked to be in his late twenties or early thirties, she thought. Close to her own age, a good-looking man in a rugged sort of way. If she didn't know better, she'd have thought he'd trimmed his hair since yesterday. It was still uncombed but did seem a little shorter, and the beard was definitely trimmer than she remembered it.

After awhile he spoke. "How's little Miss Katie doing?"

"She's getting along good with Ma." Joy was reluctant to speak of her Pa, but Jake noticed the worried expression in her eyes.

"Don't you worry none about that young'un," he said. "She's gonna do all right. Ain't nobody won't come to lovin' her with her sunshine ways."

"Yeah." Joy stood up abruptly. "Well, I got to be getting back. Ma will need help with supper."

He stretched lazily, tired from a long and busy day. "Okay, you want to drive and see how the car feels to you?" She nodded and sat in the driver's seat.

"How did you get the car turned over?" Joy asked as they headed back to Jake's farm.

"Wal, it took three of us and a horse."

"What do you mean?"

"We tied a rope to the car and to the horse. Then while Hawkins guided the horse, directin' her to pull away from the car, Jenkins and I lifted up the running board and pushed it on over."

Joy studied him for a minute. "That must've been mighty hot work."

"Wal, it weren't no picnic. She was heavier than we thought, and the horse didn't want to be pullin' like that. How's she runnin', by the way?"

"Better than when I got here," Joy said. "I really do need to pay you for all that work. Trouble is, I've gotta get a job. It'll be a while 'fore I have the money, but I'll pay you back when I can." She braked in front of his house. "Let me know how much."

Jake sat there for a moment gazing at her. Joy could feel a warm flush creep up her cheeks, and she knew the heat that generated it came from inside the car, not outside. Then Jake yawned and grinned. "You can be sure I will. And I'll let you know when I want to collect." He leaned toward her and Joy sat stone-faced as she felt his breath on her cheek. He lowered his head as if to kiss her, then suddenly drew back. "When the right time comes you'll be ready." He jumped out of the car. "Good luck with your job hunting, Joy."

She opened her eyes, which had automatically closed as he drew near. Confused at his sudden change of mood, she angrily started the car, put it in gear, and left with a quick "I'll pay you what it's worth soon's I get the money."

Joy found work at the town library keeping the shelves neat, stamping books for take-out, and putting returned books back on the shelves. Her duties also included dusting, tidying, and sweeping. She loved the mildew smell of old books and pungent furniture polish.

The town librarian, Miss O'Brien, welcomed her gladly, for she'd been hoping a younger person would come along to take her place so she could retire. She promised Joy training to be a real librarian if she proved reliable, and encouraged her to study for her high school diploma.

Miss O'Brien would help her to prepare for the test and gave her permission to study at work when things were slack. The librarian taught her how to apply for her own library card, and how to look up specific books on the shelves, even recommending some books to start with. Now that she was responsible for Katie without Stan's help, Joy began to appreciate books and learning like she'd never done in school. She became an avid reader, even bringing books home from the library for Katie to look at.

Although her salary was small, she faithfully gave a portion of it each week to her mother toward their room and board. She also set aside a tiny sum to repay Jake for fixing her car. But most of her pay she saved in a tin under her bed. This was her investment in the future for her and Katie.

Jake dropped in one Friday evening about three weeks after she'd met him. He showed up on her front porch with a part found in a junkyard for her car radio. "Thought you might like to hear a little music on your way to and from town," he said. "Won't take me a jif to put your radio together with this little jigger."

Joy was amazed that he would think of taking time for a small luxury like that. She was used to Stan's stingy ways with money and time. "What d'ya need that doodad for," he'd say. She walked out to the barn with Jake and watched while he repaired the radio. Then the two of them sat in the car and tuned in to the music of Wayne King.

"Oh, Jake, it sounds wonderful." She looked up at him, her eyes sparkling with pleasure. "The radio's never worked before. Stan was never good at fixin' things."

Jake grinned. "That music sounds pretty good. Do you like to dance?" Joy thought back to the wild dances she'd gone to with Stan, to the times he'd got so drunk he'd embarrassed her with his mean remarks, to the time she'd finally refused to go with him again. "I used to," she said, "but not anymore."

"Why not?"

"Because Stan…" She hesitated. "I just don't, that's all."

"Go on. Because Stan what? Did he embarrass you by his drinking?" She looked at him in disbelief.

"How did you…? Never mind. I don't want to talk about it." She opened the car door. "I've got to be getting in to Katie."

Jake grasped her elbow and pulled her toward him. "Wait," he said. She felt breathless as his hand sent warm tingling sensations up her arm. "I wanted to ask you to go with me to the homecoming dance this Friday," Jake said. "You don't have to dance if you don't want to. It's almost as much fun watching the others. Will you go?"

Joy hesitated. It had been months since she'd been anywhere to have fun. Yet fun was what had drawn her away with Stan, and that fun had turned out to be empty, causing more loneliness than she'd had before she'd left. She could feel the heat from Jake's hand run up her arm straight to her face, and knew she was turning red. Then suddenly making up her mind, she drew in a deep breath and said, "Yes!"

Jake beamed. "Hot dog! I'll pick you up at eight." He leaned down to kiss her, but was so excited that he missed her lips by a couple of inches and landed an exuberant kiss on her cheek.

She jumped out of the car quickly and ran toward the house. "I've got to go." She quickly disappeared through the side door, while Jake sat for a moment watching her then returned to his own vehicle.

He whistled all the way home thinking of the way her skirts flared around her ankles as she hurried back to the house, and of the way her blue eyes shimmered when she smiled.

Joy slipped into the kitchen, her cheeks burning from the touch of his lips. Did she make a mistake in agreeing to go with him to the dance? After all, she'd made a big mistake with Stan. How did she know that Jake wouldn't turn out to be a loser, too? Maybe she should send him word that she'd changed her mind, or maybe on Friday she could just tell him she was ill and couldn't go. No, that was the coward's way. Well, she'd think of something before Friday .

"What're you so red in the face for?" Joe sat at the kitchen table with his regular Friday night beer. He was on his second bottle of brew, and Joy turned to head up the back stairs, knowing how his temper rose in proportion to the amount of beer he consumed.

"I was just running up the steps, Pa."

"You sure you wasn't foolin' around with that man?" Joe was itching for an excuse to nag. His life was out of control again with a grown daughter home and a young'un in the house, and he needed to assert his authority. "I don't want him hangin' around here."

Joy whipped around and walked over to her father. She stood over him glaring into his eyes. "Pa, I'll see who I want to see. And you ain't got no call to tell me different."

Joe took a swallow of his beer. "A man's got a right to set some G.D. rules in his own house, and you won't act the tramp around my granddaughter, setting a bad example for her," he shouted.

"Momma, Momma!" Katie, alarmed by the shouting, ran up the back steps from the yard where she'd been shelling beans with her grandmother. Blanche followed at a slightly slower pace.

"Now look what you've done," Joy spoke quietly between clenched teeth. "You'll do her more harm with your shouting and meanness than Jake ever will."

She determined right then and there that she would keep her date with Jake on Friday after all.

Chapter Six

Katie burst in the door, chewing on her bottom lip as she hugged her mother's skirts and looked fearfully at her grandfather. "Momma, are you all right?"

Joy bent down and kissed her. "Yeah, baby. Grampa and I were just discussing something. It's all settled, now."

Blanche entered the kitchen. "What's all the yellin'?"

Joe slouched down in his chair, outnumbered by the women. "Nothin'," he muttered.

"That's right, it's nothin', Ma," Joy said. "Let's go outside." She smiled down at Katie. "Are you helping Grammy, Punkin?"

"Yes, Momma. We're shelling beans." Katie grinned, relieved to see her mother smile. "Come and see."

The two women and Katie returned to the back yard. They shelled quietly for several minutes, till Katie ran off to play. The women watched her for a bit, then Blanche turned to Joy. "What was that all about in there?"

"Pa was at it again, Ma. He doesn't trust me."

"What did he say?"

"Somethin about me bein' a tramp, just cuz Jake was here." Joy was angry, yet couldn't prevent a couple of tears from escaping. She wiped her cheeks with the back of her hand. "Why does he hate me?"

Blanche shook her head. "He doesn't hate you."

"Why doesn't he trust me, then?"

"It's not you. It's the trouble that might happen."

"Well, he's got to let me live my own life."

Blanche took Joy's hand and looked her in the eye. "He will, Joy. Give him time."

Joy squared her shoulders. "Well, he's not goin' to keep me from seein' who I want."

"What do you mean?"

"He's not goin' to keep me from seeing Jake, or anybody else I want."

Blanche gathered up the bean husks. "Just don't bring 'em around here too much, until he gets used to you being a woman. He still thinks of you as his little girl, and it's hard on him to see you with a young'un of your own. He don't know how to deal with it."

Katie woke up bright and early. There were a few clouds in the sky this morning, a change from the sharply etched mornings she'd experienced since the tornado. She ran to the window and looked down toward the barn. Skulking around the corner of the building, a barn cat carried something in its mouth.

Dressing quickly, Katie ran downstairs to investigate. She opened the side door, but stopped when she heard a soft, mewling sound coming from under the porch steps. Crouching down on her hands and knees, she peered under the porch. Two tiny, gray kittens huddled together on a ragged piece of blanket.

She reached in and gently drew them out. As she sat there cuddling the babies, her grandfather stepped outside on his way to the barn. "Grampa! Look what I found, two baby kittens! Can we keep 'em, please Grampa?"

Joe sat on the top step and looked down at the child. The sight stirred up a memory of Joy at about the same age with her first kitten. They'd been good friends back then. He vacillated for a moment. "I dunno," he said. "We've already got two barn cats."

"Oh please, Grampa."

"You gonna see them fed and watered?"

"Oh, yes. I'll take care of them, Grampa." She smiled up at him. "If you help me."

Joe moaned, "As if I don't have enough to do around here." He thought of how he'd failed Joy in so many ways. Maybe Fate was giving him another chance with this young'un. "Okay, Katie, but this'll be our secret. No telling your Ma or your Grammy."

Katie had set the kittens down on the blanket. Now she ran to her grandfather, her eyes glowing. "Oh thank you, Grampa. I won't tell, I promise." She jumped into his lap and planted a big kiss on his cheek, hugging him until he thought she'd choke him. "What shall we name them, Grampa?"

Joe snorted and cleared his throat, awkward with his grandchild's open affection. "Hmmph. Why don't we wait till they're a mite bigger, and we can tell 'em apart? You can be thinkin' up names in the meantime." He slid her off his lap and stood up. "Now, I can't be sitting here with you all day. I've got work to do."

"Bye, Grampa." Katie was in her own dream world hugging the kittens to her and crooning a soft lullaby.

Joe felt an unfamiliar tug in his chest as he carried with him the picture of the child bent over the kittens snuggling in her lap. He could still feel her kiss on his cheek and was surprised to feel wetness in the corners of his eyes.

Joy found she was looking forward to Friday night's date with Jake with a mixture of happy anticipation, and a sense of wariness and dread. Nevertheless, the days seemed to crawl. Katie was absorbed with the kittens, and had little time for her mother in the evenings. She'd reached some sort of peace with her grandfather, and peppered her

Grammy with questions about names for her pets. She wanted to know the names of all the animals they'd ever had.

It was Friday at last, and Joy took an early bath after supper, wanting to be fresh and clean for her evening out. Blanche had agreed to watch Katie, and Joe was in the barn fixing a straw filled bed for the kittens at Katie's request.

What can I wear to that dance, Joy stewed. She went through her clothes, a total of six dresses, and picked a flowered print in deep rose. It was old and wrinkled, but she pressed the wrinkles out with the flatiron.

Jake picked her up promptly at eight, and they left with promises to be back before midnight.

Joe stood in the barn doorway watching. He hadn't been able to bring himself out to speak to them. He knew he might lose his temper again, and he was trying to take another look at his daughter, as a woman, as Blanche had been nagging him to do. Not that he'd own up to it if she asked. He'd just keep busy, out of the way when the young man came to call. That is, unless he saw any shenanigans going on. Now as they drove away, he felt that unfamiliar tug in his chest again. Durned if the girl didn't look a good bit like her Ma had when they'd been courting. He shook his head and dove back into his carpentry project.

Joy had felt shy when she'd seen Jake all spruced up, his beard trimmed close to his chin, a clean shirt and jeans, and even his boots polished up for the occasion. He'd grinned at her in genuine appreciation of her beauty, and been a little tongue-tied himself when he'd come for her. It was Blanche who'd had to keep the conversation going, what little there was of it. Now, however, they both relaxed as the car jogged along the bumpy highway.

"Should be a good time tonight, Joy."

"I hope so. It's been a long while since I've been to anything like this."

"There'll be people there from past classes, some of them pretty old, I guess. Then there'll be some maybe from our classes too."

"I wonder if we'll know them."

"I'm sure we'll recognize some. Anyway, we'll probably meet 'em one way or another."

"What do you mean?"

"Oh, there'll be mixers planned. There usually is at these things."

Jake and Joy walked around the hall mingling with the folks who'd come to the dance. A lively fiddle or two were playing along with an accordion, and it was all Joy could do to keep her feet from tapping.

"Want to try it?" Jake asked.

"I'm not sure I know how to polka."

"It's easy, just three quick steps to each side and we spin around. I'll show you." He started off slowly until she got the hang of it, then gradually increased his speed until he was twirling her all around the dance floor. They kept bumping into other couples, the dancing space being confined. Joy proved to be a graceful dancer, picking up the steps as if she'd danced the polka all her life.

"Oh, excuse me!" She apologized to yet another couple as Jake whipped her around in a narrow space in the far corner of the room. Laughing breathlessly, she grinned up at him. "You're dangerous."

The music swung into a slow foxtrot, and he drew her closer. "Am I, Joy?" She felt his arms encircling her waist. Joy looked up at him, her face flushed. She wasn't sure if it was from the fast moving polka or from the feelings stirred up when being held in his arms. It felt good to be there, but suddenly she panicked.

"I'm hot," she said. "Can we sit this one out?"

"Sure." Jake regretfully drew apart from her and found her a chair by the door where she could get some fresh air. "I'll go get us some soda pop."

Joy watched him as he made his way through the crowd to the refreshment table. She remembered how it felt to dance close to him, the way her heart raced when he'd grinned down at her. The man was dangerous. He could snatch her heart in a twinkling if she were to give in to her attraction to him. She wasn't ready to give her heart to any man, not after the way Stan had treated her.

Although Joy had told Jake and her parents that Stan had left her, she still couldn't believe he'd gotten a divorce so quickly. She was legally free, but she wasn't ready to start cozyin' up to anyone else. She decided to keep a cool relationship between her and Jake. It was safer that way.

"Here you go." Jake returned with root beer and refreshments. They sat munching cookies and watching the couples on the dance floor. Jake pointed out one or two people he recognized from school, and some older folk he knew. Joy thought she saw three or four familiar faces. They were people who'd attended some of her high school classes, but she'd never gotten to know them and couldn't remember their names.

Suddenly the musicians called for all couples to line up on the dance floor, men on one side and women on the other. When the music started up the men were each to find a partner and dance with her.

Joy found herself dancing with a fiftyish farmer, pot-bellied and heavy of foot. He whirled her around the floor, sweat rolling down his cheeks, and told her she was the "purtiest" thing he'd laid eyes on all week.

She was relieved when the music stopped and they all had to change partners with the person next to them. This time her partner was a young man close to her own age, but all he could do for a dance step was shuffle side to side. He looked embarrassed, unable to meet her eyes. His entire concentration was on his feet, and he kept apologizing for bumping his shoe against hers.

Jake swept by with a pretty little blonde giggling up at him, her eyelashes fluttering. Joy felt a stab of pain in her stomach. *What's the matter with me? Jake can dance with whoever he wants. It doesn't matter. I'm certainly not his girl.* She couldn't be jealous. She'd already decided she wasn't going to lose her heart to Jake or any other man. They couldn't be trusted. *After all, didn't Jake just prove it? Flirting with that blonde?*

Chapter Seven

The music stopped again and this time Jake caught up to her. He was laughing as he introduced her to Betty Lou, the little blonde.

"Hi." Joy's voice was cool as she acknowledged the introduction.

"Hi yourself," Betty Lou bubbled. "You'd better keep an eye on your man here before you lose him," she giggled.

"He's not my man," Joy said stiffly.

"Oh, then you mean he's up for grabs?" Betty Lou turned to Jake. "I guess that means you and I are going to dance some more, hmmm?"

Jake disengaged his hands from Betty Lou's. He leaned down and whispered in her ear. "You'll have to excuse my wife. She and I had a little argument just before we came. You know how it is between newlyweds."

Betty Lou looked up at him in horror. "I didn't know you were married! You tricked me. I feel sorry for you," she said to Joy, and hurried off to the other side of the room.

Jake burst into laughter, and even Joy couldn't resist a giggle.

"Good riddance to that man-hunter." Jake pulled Joy close as the music started up in a dreamy waltz. "Are you having a good time, Joy?"

"I am now." Joy murmured, snuggling against him as she gave herself to the music, already forgetting she'd planned to keep her distance.

A couple of dances later, the musicians were calling for another mixer, this time a broom dance. Jake and Joy decided to opt out of this one. "I really didn't come here to give you up to the other guys," Jake said as he took her arm and guided her outside. "Let's walk awhile. It's a beautiful night, and it's hot in that crowd."

The night was mild, with no hint of autumn although September was almost past, and they knew the chill fall nights would soon be upon them.

"Is Katie settling in okay?" Jake smiled, remembering how Katie had wanted him to be her Daddy.

"She's doing a lot better since she found them kittens. Her biggest problem these days is finding names for them." Joy's thoughts drifted to the child who was the light of her life. The only good thing to come out of her marriage. And Katie was worth all the trauma of her years with Stan.

"What're you smiling at, Joy?"

"Oh, I was just thinking about Katie. It's good to see her so happy."

"You mentioned that once before, at the creek. You said something about her not havin' much fun in her life."

"Yeah, she was a scared little thing whenever she heard her Daddy yell. So she got really quiet, afraid to make him mad."

"It must be hard to have fun, when you've got to be quiet all the time."

"Yeah." Joy scuffed her shoes in the dirt path, remembering.

"What about you, Joy?"

"What about me?"

"Were you having any fun?"

She kept her head down, inspecting her shoes. "It was okay at first, but then the baby came and…" She caught herself. "Why are you askin' me these questions?" She spun around in the direction of the dance hall. "Let's go back. I've said all I'm going to say."

Jake took her arm. "Joy, I'm not asking this to pry. Well, maybe I am a little. But it's just that I want to know all about you. I don't mean no harm."

"Like I just told you, I've said all I'm goin' to say." She stepped up her pace, as anxious to get back to the dance as she was a few moments earlier to get away. Yet when they arrived back at the grange hall, she stopped abruptly outside the door.

"It's late and I've got to help Ma with the canning tomorrow. I need to be gettin' on back."

Jake was disappointed, but agreed to take her home. They rode in silence. When they reached the Russells' land, he slowed. "Joy, I'm sorry I upset you tonight, asking about your past. Will you stay out with me awhile longer? We could go park by the creek and just talk. Not about Stan," he said hastily as she made a motion for the door handle. "Please?"

Joy hesitated. She knew she should run for the house and not see him again. Yet here she was all ready to forgive him and take her chances going to the creek. Who knew what other secrets he'd pry out of her when they sat there all cozy and isolated.

What am I thinking? He's not going to pry anything out of me I don't want to tell him. The night was clear, stars plentiful in the sky, and an early harvest moon spread its golden glow across the fence posts.

"Okay, just for a little bit," she said.

When they reached the creek, the nearly full moon shone through the leaves of the cottonwoods. Its rays bounced off the surface of the brook in silvery flashes as a soft breeze rustled the leaves of the giant trees above them. They decided to walk down to the water, where they stood quietly taking in the loveliness of the scene.

"How beautiful," Joy murmured.

Jake put his arms around her, and squeezed her gently. He was silent for a moment, then he turned to study her profile. "Yes, it is beautiful."

Joy caught a softness in his tone, and stared up at the tall man beside her. She'd never seen such a tender expression on the face of any man. Not her Pa, and certainly not Stan. Her heart began to race, and she leaned toward him. Jake pulled her against him. Ever so gently he brushed his lips across her cheek, pausing at the end of her nose before claiming her lips.

Joy tentatively returned his kiss, parting her lips at the gentle probing of his tongue. The sensations that filled her were immediate and intense. She snuggled closer, needing his strength and tenderness. Jake paused between kisses only to murmur her name and she experienced a sense of cherishing she'd never before felt. Her thoughts returned to Stan, and what she now knew was a poor, cracked-mirror image of love. Yet, just remembering that relationship alarmed her, and she drew back, afraid to trust what she was experiencing with this man.

"I've got to go," she said in a panic. Turning, she scampered up the hill to the car.

"Damn," Jake muttered to himself. "She's like a frightened bird."

He stood there for a moment, getting himself under control, then followed her back to the vehicle. "What's the matter, Joy?"

"N-nothing. I've just got to get back, that's all."

Jake's eyes flashed. He started the car, not knowing if he was frustrated, or angry with himself for rushing her. "Okay, run little bird, back to your nest. You'll never learn to fly this way."

Joy's confused emotions took another nosedive at his harsh tone. "Jake, you don't understand."

"No, I don't," he answered. "You blow hot, then cold. Are you playing games with me?" Hurt by his tone as much as his words, Joy retreated, refusing to answer him. In silence they drove back to the farm.

By the time he pulled up to the porch steps, Jake had cooled down. He reached over to prevent her opening the door to hop out. "Joy, I'm sorry. I guess I was rushing you, and it's obvious you aren't ready for a deep relationship. Let's just be friends for now."

"What do you mean?"

"Wal, let's just see each other in the daytime for awhile. We can go on picnics or other daytime outings from time to time. Maybe we can take Katie with us. We can get to know each other better without your being in a panic."

"I'm not in a panic," she sputtered, reaching for the door handle.

"Joy, Joy, I know you're not right now. It's just that I'd sure enjoy your company, and I don't want you going away mad." He grinned at her. "What d'ya say. Can we begin again? Will you go on a picnic with me next weekend?"

Despite herself, Joy's heart softened at his boyish smile. "When?" she asked.

"How about next Sunday afternoon? I'll bring the beans."

"Oh, and what am I gonna have to bring?"

"Just yourself...And some dessert...And chicken and veggies, if you don't mind."

Her resistance melted at the twinkle in his eye, and his cheeky boldness at requesting the food. "Okay, then. I guess it will be all right, but I'm bringin' Katie along."

"Of course," he said, happy that she'd agreed to see him again. "Didn't I say Katie, too? I reckon I wouldn't have it any other way." With that, he released the door handle. He walked around to Joy's door just as she climbed out of the car, not waiting for him to open it. "Goodnight, Joy," he said, squeezing her hand, and turning back to the vehicle.

"Thanks for tonight," she replied. "I had a good time at the dance." She retreated into the house, confused that he hadn't tried to kiss her again.

Jake drove home wondering if the only good time she'd had tonight was at the dance.

Katie was excited about the picnic. "Can I please bring my kittens, Momma," she asked at least three times a day.

"If you don't quit asking, you'll be stayin' home with them," Joy finally told her. "We are not going to have to worry about them kittens getting lost."

At last the big day arrived. Jake picked them up in his truck. It was a warm Indian summer day, the humidity of August and September having given way to a dryer more comfortable heat.

"Where are we going, Mr. Jake?" Katie asked after they got the food basket stowed away in the back, and the three of them settled in their seats. Jake grinned at them.

"It's a surprise," he answered.

"Oh, boy!" Katie bounced up and down, trying to see out the window and guess where they were going. "Is it at the creek?"

"No."

"At your house?"

"No."

"In town?"

"No. Now your three guesses are up."

"Yes, Katie." Joy said. "For heaven's sake, be still awhile and watch out the window. We'll be there before you know it. Let's enjoy the ride."

"Here, I'll turn on the radio," Jake said. He found a country station and they were soon singing along with the music. Just before reaching the town of Pennnywhistle, he turned off on a narrow country road. They drove a few miles, and the road turned into gravel. It was too bumpy after that to sing. Katie slid back and forth on the seat, which sent her into fits of laughter. Before long, Jake pulled over onto a grassy strip and parked. "All out. We're here," he said. They spilled out of the car and looked around. A grove of trees stood beside the car, bright with the colors of autumn.

They wandered through the trees and came out onto a grassy hill sloping gently down to the Kanasockett River, which widened at this point in its journey, bubblng over rocks and around fallen tree limbs. In the distance they could see the slightly rolling hills of northeastern Kansas alive with the persimmon and pumpkin colors of the season.

"Oh, it's so pretty here!" Joy stood spellbound.

"Momma, Momma! Can I go in the water?" Katie ran down toward the river.

"No, Katie!" Joy raced to stop the little girl before she ran in over her head.

"Hold it, Katie." Jake caught up to her. "Let's unload the car, then we'll take a walk and check out this place. Maybe we'll find a special place for you to go in."

They walked back to the car, then carried the picnic things over to a big, flat rock under a large shade tree where Joy spread a cloth. After placing their baskets on the rock they returned to the riverbank. Jake showed them where the water flowed over some larger rocks in a gurgling waterfall upstream. Katie hunted for smooth stones and Jake showed her how to skip them across the water.

There were a few small pieces of driftwood, bleached out by the sun. Joy found one twisted so it resembled a bird, which she decided to take home with her. They discovered a shallow beach, and Katie was allowed to wade in the water. After an hour or so, Jake said, "I'm hungry. What d'ya say we go have our picnic?"

All were hot and thirsty by the time they got back to their rock. Joy poured them each a cup of lemonade from the jug she'd brought, and passed out the fried chicken and salad. Jake served his homemade beans and cornbread. When they'd stuffed themselves, he sat back and said, "I don't know when I've had a better meal."

"Wait'll you see the dessert Momma made," Katie told him. "Momma makes the bestest cake."

"Is that right, Miss Kate?" Jake grinned at her, glad to see her so happy. "Well, Joy, when do we get to see this great and wonderful cake?"

"It's just a simple cake, really, but Katie loves it," Joy said, opening the cake dish.

"That's because it's got jam in it," Katie said. "Momma gave me a tiny cake just like it when she made this one."

"Oh, so you got a sample ahead of time, huh? I guess that means I get to have two pieces." Jake tweaked Katie's braid.

"You're right," he said a little while later as he licked jam off his fingers. "Your Momma makes the bestest cake!"

Joy blushed, and busied herself with cleaning up the leftovers. Once the picnic things were picked up and replaced in the car, they hiked further up the river, eventually coming to a pretty little forest glade just opposite the falls. They propped themselves against a tree to listen to the water, and Jake told them stories of his childhood when he'd first discovered this paradise. After awhile, Katie, warmed by the sun, fell asleep.

"She's had such a fun time today," Joy said. "Thank you for making it so special for her."

"Well, she's a special youngster, not a bit of trouble. I can't understand how her Daddy could run off and not want to see you two again."

Joy squirmed for a minute, then made up her mind to confide in him. "Stan wrote me. He sent some papers. I guess we're legally divorced now."

Jake looked at her, his eyes questioning. "How do you feel about that?"

"Well, there's never been a divorce in my family before. Pa like to hit the roof when he knew it was all over between us, but I know I couldn't go on forever the way things were. 'Specially for Katie's sake. She's much happier with her grandparents." Joy stood up. "Tell me again how you found this place."

Jake grinned, knowing she was purposely changing the subject. He was pleased she had trusted him enough to share this much, and secretly was happy that she was now free. "I used to come out here when I was a boy to hunt possum," he began. They walked slowly along the riverbank. Jake continued to talk of the land. "This is where I dreamed I'd build my house someday."

"Do you own the land?" Joy asked.

"No. I saved up my army pay, and put a little aside from other jobs I've taken on. Now I've almost got enough saved to buy this piece. Just have to convince the owner that I'm the man to care for it."

"When are you going to do that?"

"Wal, I've been sort of waitin' till the right woman comes along to share it with me." Jake's eyes twinkled as he grinned at her.

Joy looked quickly away, her face growing warm and flushed. "Well, I hope you find the one you're looking for pretty soon."

"Oh, I already have." He beamed at her.

*Could it be...*Joy quickly rose to her feet, her heart pounding. *No, Jake can have any woman he wants. Some pretty woman like that Betty Lou he was havin' fun with at the dance. Why would he want me?"* Good," she said. "Well, I think we've been here long enough. Katie, wake up. We've got to be getting on home."

"Wait. Don't you want to know who I'm thinking of?"

"No, that's your business, Mister. C'mon, Katie."

The little girl rolled over and stretched. "Where are we going, Momma?"

"It's time to go home. Get your sweater on, and let's start back to the truck."

"Joy, what's your hurry, and what's this Mister bit again?" Jake asked, puzzled by her sudden change of mood.

"It's late. I can't be out here lollygaggin' all day. There's work to be done at home."

"But...!" It was no use. Joy was already half a dozen steps ahead of him, pulling Katie along with her. He stood there staring after her, scratching his head in frustration. "Durned woman. Running away again. Now what did I do or say to spook her?"

Chapter Eight

Jake loped after them and soon caught up. Taking Joy's arm, he spun her around. "Joy, slow down. Let's enjoy this place a little longer."

Katie by this time was almost at their picnic rock. "Momma, can we *please* stay here a little bit longer?"

Joy looked at the two pleading faces before her and sighed. "Okay, Katie. Just a few minutes, though."

Katie ran down to sit on a log she'd found earlier near the water. Here she'd placed a few smooth rocks she'd found and wanted to take home with her. Joy and Jake sat once more on the picnic rock. For several minutes they sat quietly and watched the little girl at play. Finally Jake broke the silence. "Why did you run away from me, Joy?"

"What do you mean?"

"Just now, when we were talking, you just up and left. Did I say something to make you mad?"

"No." Joy looked away. She wasn't sure herself why she'd run, only she knew it had to do with the fact he'd told her he'd found a woman, and she didn't want to stick around to find out who it was. She figured he'd brought her here to tell her so she wouldn't think he'd be coming around anymore.

Well, she could get along just fine without him. She'd never even known him before the past couple months, and she'd gotten along without him then, hadn't she? Why then, did she feel so sick at her stomach?

"Well, if you're not mad, then couldn't we keep on enjoying the day together?" Jake bent down to look her in the eye, and Joy raised her head to find she was staring at his lips, just inches away from her own. With a groan, Jake drew her into his arms and nibbled at her lips. Then pulling her tighter, he kissed her soundly.

She felt a warm tingling shoot through her as she opened up to his kiss. She knew she'd never felt this tenderness and rapture with Stan. She sighed against him and gave herself up to his caresses with enthusiasm and ardor. But only for a moment. Suddenly she drew back and stared at him. "We've got to go. You take me home right now, Mister Jake."

He stared at her, dazed from the fervor of their shared passion. When he saw that she meant it, he pulled himself together quickly and stood scowling at her. "All right, **Miss** Joy. We're going." Jake strode toward the car, leaving her to collect Katie and stumble after him. Puzzled and angry when he left her so abruptly, she said nothing more to him as they got into the car.

The ride back was much quieter than the trip out to the picnic spot had been. Katie sensed the tension and asked, "Are you mad, Mr. Jake?"

He looked down at the girl, knowing something of the violence and anger she'd faced in her short life. Abruptly he stopped the car, and hugged her to him. "No, Katie. I'm not mad. I was just feeling a little lonely, that's all." Jake and Joy exchanged glances over Katie's head, and he smiled sadly. "Forgive me?" he mouthed.

Joy was more baffled than ever. This man didn't fit her notions and experience of what men were like. She couldn't hold anger toward anyone who treated her daughter so special. She nodded.

Katie snuggled into the hug "You shouldn't be lonely, Mr. Jake. You've got us now, huh Momma?"

"Uh…" Joy was at a loss to respond, but Jake quickly started the car.

"Thank you, Katie. I'm glad you and your Momma are my friends." He turned the radio on and bellowed out a tune along with the country singer. Soon all three were harmonizing again. When Katie fell asleep in the back seat, Jake reached over and squeezed Joy's hand. "Have fun, today?" he asked.

She snuggled against his shoulder. "Mmm-hmm, it was a good day," she answered.

Katie awoke just as they pulled into the farmyard. She couldn't wait to tell her Grammy all about her day. With a goodbye hug for Jake, she ran for the steps and disappeared into the house.

Jake smiled down at Joy and drew her close. He kissed her forehead, then nibbled on her ear, and finally his warm and exciting lips claimed hers. She felt that kiss all the way down to her belly.

How can it feel so good, she wondered, *just to be kissed by this man?* When Stan kissed her, oh, it had felt pretty good at first, but then he'd pawed at her breasts at the same time, and his kisses began to sicken her. *Maybe it was because he was so rough*, she 'spected. Jake pulled her close and turned up the music a bit. She snuggled against his shoulder. Sammy Kaye's Swing poured out of the little car radio and they sat listening.

"It's so peaceful, here," Jake said.

"Yeah, don't you wish it could always be like this?" Joy answered. "I wish…"

"What do you wish?"

"I don't know—just that things could be different, that Katie could have had a good Daddy…I dunno, just—things, I guess."

"It sounds like it must've been pretty hard for Katie."

"Yeah, it was hard for both of us."

"Do you want to talk about it?" His lips whispered kisses on her forehead and she melted against him. He would be so easy to talk to, she thought.

Making up her mind, she began. "We was hungry a lot, but he didn't want me to get work in a diner, like I used to. Said he wasn't going to have anyone think he couldn't take care of his wife."

"Sounds like he wanted to take care of you himself, then."

"Yeah, only…"

"Only what?"

"Only, when he did get money he didn't want to give us much for food or clothes. He needed it, he said."

"Maybe he owed somebody."

"Maybe, but…"

"But what?"

"He used to spend it on beer and whiskey. If he had any extra, he'd go play cards all night. It got so I was happier when he didn't have any extra money."

"Why, Joy?"

"Cause he'd get so drunk, and he'd leave us all night. Then when he'd come home, he'd…"

"What?"

"He'd get mad at everything and he'd…" She ducked her head and cringed, remembering how it was.

Jake lifted her chin. "What, Joy? He didn't hit you, did he?"

"Sometimes," she admitted, shamed. She dropped her head down and couldn't look at him again. "And he always told me I was no good, that I couldn't do anything right."

Jake took her face in both of his hands and gently lifted her head till she looked into his eyes. "Joy, you're worth a hundred thousand times more than that man. Don't ever believe that pack o' lies." He gazed at her with such obvious caring that she blushed and lowered her eyes once again. "Don't you believe me, Joy?" he asked.

"Yes, I guess so." she mumbled.

"Good." He beamed at her. "Now, come here, and let me prove it to you." He held her in his arms and gently kissed her cheeks, her nose, her forehead, her lips. Joy was filled with a special tenderness toward this man.

She sat back and smiled at him. "Now it's your turn."

"My turn?"

"Your turn to tell me about Jake. You said you were in the army, then came home after a couple of years. What did you do then?"

Jake sat quietly for a moment. He'd never discussed the tragedy that had taken away his young wife, and he found it difficult now. "I came back to Enterprise and married the girl I fell in love with in high school."

Joy's stomach clenched and she felt as if he had stabbed her right square in the heart. "Y-you're married?"

Jake stared straight ahead, then closed his eyes in remembrance. "No, she's dead."

He looked so sad that Joy could only feel compassion for him. She squeezed his hand. "Oh Jake, I'm so sorry. Do you want to tell me about it?"

"Vivian and I dated all through our junior and senior years. When I joined the Army, we promised to wait for each other. It was Vivian who made Army life bearable. She wrote to me every Sunday. I sure looked forward to those letters."

"They must have seemed like a visit home," Joy murmured.

"Yeah. Well, I didn't know how I was gonna support a wife when I got free of the Army, but I was willing to do anything to have her. When my hitch was over I came back to town. She met me at the train station, and she was every bit as beautiful as when I'd left, even more so." Jake was lost in his memories now and hardly aware of Joy beside him.

"My first night back we sat on her porch for hours, catching up on all the town news and dreamin' of our future."

He paused, sitting on that porch once again in memory. "Go on," Joy urged, sensing his need to talk about his loss.

"About midnight, Vivian's Daddy came out to hint it was time for me to leave. We said goodnight while he waited there in the doorway. Vivian went inside and I turned to go, but her Daddy called me back.

"'What are your plans?' he asked me. I told him I wanted to find a job, and that I hoped to marry his daughter, if she'd have me.

"'Well, young man,' he says to me. 'I don't think you have anything to worry about there. Vivian's never looked at another man since you left. And as far as a job, that's what I want to talk to you about. How'd you like to work in the store?' He owned a big department store over in Pennywhistle, and was looking for someone to train to take over when he retired. Since he had no sons he hoped to bring his daughter's husband into the business. Keep it in the family, so to speak."

"And did you take his offer?"

"Well, I'm an outdoor man myself, but work was scarce in these parts, I knew, and like I said, I'd do anything to have Vivian as my wife. So yes, I agreed, and a week later I was fully employed and engaged to be married."

"Go on."

"We had one and a half wonderful years. She was expecting our first child, about eight months along..." Here Jake faltered. He sat there staring out the window. Joy waited, sensing his tension. After a moment or two he took a deep breath and continued.

"One night I was working late at the store. She was driving home from a visit to her parents. She had some difficulty moving quickly with her stomach big from her child. It had been snowing for an hour or so, and the wind was blowing in a gale force. The flakes were big and thick. She came to a railroad crossing, and they think the car was either stuck on the track or just that she couldn't get it to move fast over them."

"Oh, Jake," Joy breathed, caught up in his story.

He stared into her eyes, and mumbled. "They say it was quick. She never even felt it. The train was going sixty miles an hour." He put his head down on her shoulder and sobbed as if his heart were breaking all over again.

Joy reached out and pulled him into her arms, weeping right along with him. "Oh, Jake, how horrible for you." They sat there for several minutes until Jake's great racking sobs diminished and he pulled out his handkerchief.

"Afterwards her father sold the store. He had no heart for it anymore, and her parents moved away to live out west nearer to their older daughter."

"Did you quit the store then, too?"

"No, I stayed on for about six months. I had to keep on going or I'd have gone crazy. At least while I was at the store I was busy enough to keep from thinking for awhile. But the nights were terrible. I wasn't getting any sleep. Finally I just up and quit. I started workin' for a rancher outside of Pennywhistle. He worked us hard and long, which was what I needed. Being outdoors was healin' for me, and I was so tired after the physical labor I began to sleep nights again. I saved all my money, 'cause I didn't want to spend it drinking and gambling with the other cowboys. When the Grant place came up for lease I decided to take it and try my hand at farming. It was a good decision."

He pulled her against him and kissed the top of her head. "Now enough about me. We were talking about how you're worth so much more than that worthless husband had you thinkin'. I believe I was provin' that to you," he smiled and cuddled her close, his lips once again seeking hers.

When they both stopped for breath, he grinned down at her. "See? You're worth more than I can say, Joy. Thanks for listening to my story. I've never told anyone before." He took her hand and squeezed it. "Now we'd better say good-night before I get carried away and whisk you off to my hide-away."

Stan staggered to the bedroom, one hand clutching his beer, face beet red and eyes blurred from all the booze he'd downed that evening. He squinted at the letter in his other hand.

Chrissake, he raged. *That old bag has a nerve. Who does she think she is, tellin' me to get out. Just 'cause I'm a little behind in my rent. Three months is nothin'. She oughta be glad I'm here and the place ain't vacant, ripe fer squatters. Hell and damnation. Proves it. Women ain't fit fer nothin' but a roll in the sack.* He heaved his empty bottle across the room where it missed the bed. Headache pounding, he grimaced when he heard the shatter of glass as it sailed on through the window.

Christ, now she'll have the police here claiming damages as well as rent. Where the hell was he going to get any money to live on, now they'd thrown him out of his job. *Just cause I beat the shit outta that mama's boy Eddie Weinberg. Damn moron, where does he get off tryin' to tell me how to do my work.*

He decided he'd better get out before the landlady came back with the cops, so stuffed his few clothes into an old leather bag and took one last look around the room. *Nothin' but a dump, anyways.* He grabbed his last two bottles of beer, jammed them on top of his clothes and left the apartment without a backward glance. Hiking over to the tracks, he caught the 5AM freight heading east. By eleven he'd arrived in his old hometown of Enterprise and stashed his bag beneath some underbrush near the tracks.

Stan swaggered into the Hungry Bear and over eggs and coffee sweet-talked the waitress into telling him what he'd hoped to learn. Joy had a job working in the town library, and his old friend Hank Abrams was still in town. He'd con Joy into giving him some of her pay, steady like, and he'd hole up with his old drinking buddy.

He tossed a few coins on the counter and walked down Main Street till he found Hank's old man's garage. Kicking the feet sticking out from under a '34 Hudson, he was rewarded with a string of curses. The man under the car came up spitting mad till he saw who was standing there.

"Stan, you old so'n so. When did you blow into town?" They pounded each other on the shoulders.

"Hiya, Hank. Just this mornin'. Hey, ol' buddy. Ya still got that ol' fishin' shack?"

"Yeah. Matter of fact, I live there. Why?"

"Well, I was lookin' fer a place to hang out. Just temporary, you understand."

"Hell, this sounds like a deal fer us to discuss over a beer. Why don't ya meet me out there in a couple hours?"

"Will do, ol' man." Stan tramped around town for awhile, then moseyed on over to the library to see if he could see Joy. She wasn't working but the old bag running the show told him what he wanted to know. He quickly learned Joy's hours and decided he'd pay her a visit later after he'd worked out a place to stay.

Bored with town, he picked up his gear from down by the tracks and ambled out to the shack. On the edge of town he passed a small house set back from the road, surrounded by a chain link fence. As he dawdled along, a baseball soared over the fence and just missed his left ear. "Mister, mister," yelled two small boys. "Can you get the ball for us?" Stan grinned. Why not, he had nothin' better to do at the moment. Anyways, he remembered when he was a half pint he'd had his share of lost balls, and they were hard to come by. He scrambled across the road and rescued the ball from a grove of nettles. Winding up his pitching arm, he let fly a curved ball that dropped right in front of the small pitcher. "Wow! Did you see that?" the little boy said to his brother. "Mister, do you want to play ball with us?" he yelled to Stan.

"Naw, but thanks." With a wave, Stan continued on his way. *That little guy was awright,* he thought. *Too bad Katie wasn't a boy. I might have kept her around.* When he got to Hank's shanty he downed his last two beers, sacked out on the mattress and was soon sawing logs.

"What the hell?" Dreaming of a train crash, his body rolling and shaking, Stan found himself dumped out of bed and on to the floor with a grinning Hank above him, bottle of beer in one hand and a fifth of whiskey in the other.

"On your feet, ol' friend. We've got some serious drinkin' to do."

The two men bragged on their drinking scrapes in high school and their struggles to survive the tight years since. Hank had never married, but had some gal he visited over in Pennywhistle whenever he had a few bucks to spend. Stan envied him his freedom all these years. "Hell, livin' with the little woman ain't all it's cracked up to be. They want you home every night, lose all their fun-lovin' ways. Joy just kept sayin' she wanted security. Specially when the brat came along." He downed another swig of whiskey. "I'm well shed o' her. Now I don't have to answer to anyone."

"I'll drink to that." Hank grabbed the bottle, tipped it on end for a gulp, dribbling a portion of it down his chin. He wiped it away with his sleeve. "Hey, ol frien', whattaya say we visit my girl over in Pennywhistle? She's got a red-headed gal friend who's real fine." He nudged Stan and winked. "I'm sure you two'll hit it off jest great."

"What are we waitin' for?" Stan lurched to his feet. "I can wait till tomorrow to take care of my business here in town. Guess I'll go make myself bee-u-ti-ful!" They slapped each other on the back and lurched outside to pee off the back step.

Joy worked hard all morning rearranging some of the bookshelves and creating a special display. Every now and then she'd feel her skin crawl and she'd look suddenly over her shoulder. She felt as though someone was watching her, but she couldn't figure out who.

There were always five or six people at a time in the library. Whenever she glanced in their direction they seemed to be busy browsing the shelves or reading, yet sometimes when she'd go down one aisle she'd get the impression someone was just disappearing around a corner to the next. By lunchtime she couldn't wait to get out of there and over to the Hungry Bear.

Even in the restaurant she felt as though she were sitting in a fish bowl, someone inspecting her, ready to stick her with a fish hook. She talked for awhile to the waitress, but couldn't shake her edgy feelings. Yet whenever she scanned the restaurant she saw only a few local customers studying the menu, chatting with each other, or busy eating their lunch. No one seemed to be paying any attention to their surroundings much less noticing her.

She thought of Stan and how he'd often made her feel this same creepy feeling when he'd been drinking heavy. He'd come into the bedroom where she pretended to be asleep. Standing over her for a minute or two he'd leer down at her until she'd feel her skin crawl, then he'd flop on the bed and pounce on her. Now she wondered why she was thinking of him and why she felt that he was somehow around. He couldn't be. Stan left her a long way from here. Besides, he'd always said he hated this town, so why would he come back? No, he couldn't be anywhere near Enterprise.

Hank and Stan were gleeful as they compared notes on stalking Joy. "She'll be ready to pay me off just to get us off her back," Stan howled, slapping his knee.

Chapter Nine

The snowflakes swirled in the gusting winds like the autumn leaves had only a few weeks earlier. Joe came in from the barn, stamping his boots, sending watery rivulets across the back-entry floor. He stripped off his gloves and jacket, tossed his knitted hat in the direction of the clothes tree, and sat at the kitchen table.

He'd been out in the unseasonal snow for hours, it seemed, trying to finish the roof over the chicken house, and in general complete the repair of the outbuildings in preparation for winter weather. Blanche put down the sweater she was knitting for Katie, and went to the stove where she'd been keeping the teakettle hot. She poured the boiling water onto a tea bag in a mug, and brought it to him.

Joe almost burned his tongue, from drinking it quickly to lift the chill.

"Don't know when I've seen such a storm so early in the year," he said. "Hope it don't mean we're in for a hard winter." He sneezed, an eruption from the depths of his being, then sneezed twice again. "How about another cup of tea, Blanche," he mumbled as he moved over by the fire. "I can't seem to get warm." Blanche fixed a second cup and took it to him.

As she passed him the mug their hands touched, and she felt his heat. Concerned, she placed her hand on his forehead. "Joe, you're burning up! Why'd you stay out in that cold so long?"

"What d'ya 'spect me to do? I didn't see nobody else out there to help me get it done," he growled. "Them animals wouldn'ta made it through the night if I didn't get 'em squared away." He continued to shiver. "Put some of yer cookin' brandy in this here tea, Blanche. That oughta warm me up."

Blanche opened her mouth to argue, then changed her mind. It could be the brandy would help. At least it would maybe give him a good night's rest, which couldn't do no harm. She took down the bottle and poured an ounce or two into his cup.

"Thanks," he grunted, then sipped on the drink, silently staring into the fire. "Where's Joy and Katie?" he said finally.

"Joy's upstairs studying. Katie's gone to sleep already. She was tired after playing in the snow all afternoon."

"She seems to be gettin' along all right."

"What do you mean?"

"I guess I mean she seems to have settled in."

"Well, with her grampa spoiling her, why wouldn't she?"

"What d'ya mean spoilin' her?"

"Letting her have not one, but two cats, and then takin' 'em up to her room every night. Making them a special bed." Blanche could see how Katie had gotten around her blustery grandfather a little more every day. "Even giving her a ride on the horse, and her still such a little tyke."

"Blanche, I've told you b'fore, an' I'll tell ya again. You worry too much." He sneezed again, a deep belly-wrenching explosion, shaking the cup in his hand till the spiked tea spattered over the sides. "Damn! Hope I'm not gettin' a cold. I'm going to bed. Lock up, will ya, Blanche? You comin' up?"

Blanche shook her head. "No, I believe I'll set here awhile and work on this sweater." She listened as his footsteps dragged up the stairs and thought about the changes the last couple months had brought. She and Joe were speaking again. Oh not much, but at least they had Joy and Katie to talk about.

There still wasn't any love lost between them, but Joe didn't seem to be drinking as much beer, certainly not flying into rages or passing out. And things were a lot more peaceful without that.

He and Joy seemed to have reached some kind of truce, too. Joy kept her head buried in books these days, or else she and that young man of hers would take Katie on an outing. So she really wasn't around too much for Joe to pick on.

Blanche thought about Katie. The little girl seemed happier and had even filled out a bit. Blanche saw to that with her hot biscuits, which the child loved, and her potatoes and gravy. She wrapped the afghan around her more tightly as she heard the wind rattle the shutters.

Joe didn't look good tonight. Hope he weren't going to be too sick to do the chores. She'd done them for him in the past, but didn't relish going out in this weather to tend to the animals. Oh well. She shrugged her shoulders, thinking *I guess we'll make it through if he does get sick. It won't be the first time life is hard.* Finishing her row, she put the knitting down, added another log to the fire and closed up the house for the night.

Joe arose chilled to the bone. He dressed quickly, stoked up the fire in the kitchen stove, and went out to care for the animals. The snow had blown into drifts as high as the porch rail. Retreating into the back entry, he spoke to Blanche who was making hot oatmeal. "Goldern snow is coverin' the porch. I'm gonna have to dig my way to the barn." He grabbed the shovel and headed back out.

"Wait, Joe, eat some hot breakfast first." Blanche's words were useless, as the door slammed shut behind him.

Joe shoveled hard for close to an hour before the path was cleared. At last stopping to rest, he felt a chill shake him from head to toe. "Durn cold comin' on," he muttered, as he hurried to feed the animals.

When he'd finished his chores he trudged back into the house, shedding his coat and boots in the entryway. He stood by the fire shivering and feeling slightly dizzy. Blanche poured a cup of black coffee and took it to him, then placed a bowl of oatmeal on the kitchen table. "Joe, you're pale as a ghost. Here, sit down and eat."

"I'm all right, just got a chill. I'll feel better once I get my belly full."

"Joy's not gonna get to work this morning. The road'll be impassable," Blanche told him. "I've been listening to the radio. The plows aren't ready for winter, and there's only one operating."

"At that rate, it'll be tomorrow before the road's open." Joe finished his breakfast and returned to the living room, sitting in his easy chair near the potbelly stove where Blanche had built a fire.

"Joy's got to get to work somehow," she said. "They're in the middle of reorganizin' a whole section of the library, and they can't just leave those books all piled up like that."

Just then Joy came down for breakfast. "I've gotta get to town," she said. "Pa, are those old snowshoes still out in the barn?"

"Yeah, but you'll never make it on them. It would take you all day to git there. Besides, they need some repairin' 'fore they'd be usable."

Katie, still in her pajamas, appeared in the doorway and ran shivering over to the fire. "Momma, can I go snow-shoeing with you?"

"Not today, baby, it's too far, and you'd be all tuckered out b'fore we got half-way there. Pa, can't you make the repairs this mornin'? I can short-cut over the fields, and get some work in anyways."

Before Joe could answer, there was a knock at the kitchen door. Joy opened it to find Jake standing there. "I hitched up my sleigh and came over to see if you need a ride to work."

Joy stepped back into the kitchen. "Oh no," she said, not wanting to be beholden to him again. "I'm fixin' to use snowshoes."

Joe overheard her and hollered from the living room. "Joy, I told you those shoes need fixin'!"

"What d'ya say, then, Joy?" Jake asked, grinning down at her.

She was firm. "Jake, I don't want you to be goin' out of your way to get me to town."

The grin faded. "Look, *Miss* Joy. It so happens I'm headed in to town anyways to pick up some extra feed. Now if you'd climb down off yer high horse, we could share a ride and make a pleasant trip of it."

"Momma, Momma, can I go with you?" Katie gave Jake a bear hug. "Please, Mr. Jake. Can I go on a sleigh ride too?"

Joy looked at the hopeful faces of Jake and her daughter and relented. "Come in, Jake. Looks like the only way I'm gonna get to work is to go with you. Katie, go get dressed, and if you're ready when

I am, you can go. Jake, you might as well get you a cup of coffee while I have my breakfast. Have you ate yet?"

Jake took off his jacket and hat. Stomping his snow-covered boots in the entry, he removed them and poured himself a mug of coffee. Joy sat down with a bowl of oatmeal while he pulled up a chair and helped himself to a slice of toast. Katie in the meantime raced back upstairs and returned in record time fully dressed. She joined them at the table and gulped down her cereal, chattering about the snow and asked Jake to help her build a snowman.

"When we get back if it's still light out," he promised.

Bundled up in her last year's winter jacket and some old boots from Joy's childhood, Katie ran outside and gave the horses each a carrot. Jake came out and boosted her up to the sleigh and Joy climbed up beside her.

Inside, Blanche busied herself cleaning up the breakfast dishes. When finished, she sat in the rocking chair by the fire and picked up her knitting. Joe turned on the radio to a dance music station, then got his knife from the back entry and some pieces of wood he'd been saving for the winter. He sorted through them and picked out a piece twice as long as it was wide, then sat at the kitchen table. "Guess this'll do." He began chiseling away.

"What're you going to make, Joe?" Blanche hadn't seen him do his wood carving since Joy had left.

"Somethin' for Katie for Christmas. I dunno if it'll turn out to be anything, it's been so long since I've done any whittlin'." Blanche looked over at Joe. He was digging away at the block of wood, his forehead scrunched up in furrows like a newly planted cornfield. It was nice, she thought, to have him sitting with her, him carving his wood and her knitting. Almost like the early, happier years of their marriage.

"Whee!" Katie hollered as they set off with her ringing the sleighbells as hard as she could shake them. She chattered all the way to town and there was no opportunity for private conversation between Jake and Joy.

"Thanks for the ride," Joy said as she stood on the sidewalk in front of the library.

"Glad to do it. I'll be back about lunchtime and we can eat at the *Hungry Bear.*"

Joy worked steadily all morning, removing books from their shelves, and stacking them in piles across the room. Katie helped carry some of them. When she got bored with that she looked at picture books, or played with some blocks and the few other toys that were kept in a corner of the library.

There were only three customers on this chilly day, just people returning books that were due. Miss O'Brien, the librarian, left about eleven, sneezing and sniffling. She told Joy she was going to take to her bed, and that if it stayed slow after lunch Joy could close up as soon as she finished. With no one needing help in choosing or locating books, Joy spent most of her time getting the books back on the shelves in their new locations. Jake returned about noon, and took them to the small family diner on Main Street. Katie was thrilled to sit in a booth with them and have a hot bowl of vegetable soup.

"Well, looks like this snowstorm might keep us from havin' a picnic Saturday like we planned. I have another idea though." Jake spoke quickly seeing Katie's disappointment. "The radio says this here's a freak storm and should melt in a couple of days. How about we ride over to Pennywhistle on Saturday and see the Christmas decorations that are already up in the stores? We could walk around town for a bit and then see a movie."

"Me too?" Katie asked, bouncing in her seat, and nearly spilling her soup.

"What d'ya say, Joy?" Jake grinned. "Katie, too?"

"It sounds like a great idea, but we still have to eat," Joy said. "We'll go if you come have lunch at the house first."

Jake looked hesitant. "Don't you think that will bother your Pa?"

"I've got a right to ask someone to lunch." Joy scowled.

"Well, if it doesn't cause no problem with your Pa and Ma, I'll come. But if they don't take to the idea, we'll eat something in the car on the way to Pennywhistle."

Joy stood up. "We'll see. Now I've got to get back to work."

Jake paid the bill and they returned to the library. "When do you want to head back home, Joy?"

"Probably in another couple hours."

"Why don't I take Katie with me? I promised to drop off some feed at my neighbor Hawkins' house. Katie can see his new dog."

"I don't know...I wouldn't want her to be a bother to you." Joy was hesitant, so used to caring for Katie or leaving her with Blanche that she couldn't imagine anyone else watching her.

"Heck, she's no bother. She's good company," Jake responded. "Besides, you'll probably get done faster without her getting in your way."

"Well, Katie...do you want to go with Mr. Jake to see Mr. Hawkins' new dog?"

"Yeah, Momma!" Katie ran to put on her coat.

"We'll pick you up about three," said Jake. Joy worked hard on the books after they left, noting that Jake was right and she accomplished more in a shorter time without Katie's interruptions. She stooped down to place a heavy book on a lower shelf, when she heard a chilling and familiar mocking laugh.

Chapter Ten

"Well if it ain't sweet Joy. So you got you a job." Stan stood over her, his hat at a rakish angle. He wore a heavy field coat, unbuttoned, over a worn flannel shirt. His cigarette stub was held in nicotine stained fingers peeking out through holes in his gloves.

"What are you doing here?" Joy asked as she jumped up in dismay.

"Well, I'm mighty glad you asked me that. You see, I need a little cash to tide me over you might say."

"I don't have any money for you. I have all I can do to take care of Katie as it is."

"Ah yes, sweet, sweet Kate. Where is she by the way?"

"Never mind, she's being taken care of," Joy said quickly, praying that Jake and Kate wouldn't come back until Stan had gone.

"Well, it don't matter, nohow. I can always find her and I'll see her if I want to." He leered at her.

Joy couldn't believe she had ever been attracted by his smile. Now it totally repulsed her. "You leave her alone."

"Oh, you want to make sure I do?" Glaring at her, he brought his fist down on the desk so hard it sounded like a gunshot. "Then you'd better come up with some money."

"I don't have any money for you," she cried, springing back in alarm.

"I happen to know you get paid tomorrow, Joy. I'll give you till four. You can meet me over at the Hungry Bear. A man's got to have his dinner, now don't he?"

"I can't give you money." Joy was desperate. "I have to pay Ma and Pa for rent, and have some left over for Katie. She's outgrowing all her clothes."

"Well now, you're such a good little homebody, I'm sure you can find something of yours to cut down for her. You don't need party dresses anymore, now do you? That is, unless you're running around again with somebody. You always were a party girl, weren't you?" He held up his right hand as if to ward off a blow. "Course that's not important right now. You just be sure you're at the Hungry Bear tomorrow with all your pay." With an icy glare he turned on his heel and left.

Joy sat down at the desk, her head in her hands and sobbed. "What am I going to do?" She knew Stan would carry out his threat and find Katie and even take her away if she didn't give him money. But how was she to do it and save for her and Katie's future? She stewed as different alternatives occurred to her.

She and Katie could run away, somewhere where he couldn't find her. But she didn't have enough money saved for that. And she'd have no job and no one to mind Katie if she did get work. She knew Jake would help her if she let him, but there was no way she would involve him in her affairs. No, she'd have to figure out something else.

Tomorrow she'd give Stan what she'd saved under her bed, but there was no way she would miss giving part of her pay to Ma, or skip paying Jake what she owed him for fixing her car.

She'd talked to the man at the automotive garage. He'd given her an estimate of what he would've charged to get her car turned right side up and working again after the tornado, and she was determined to pay Jake that amount. With tomorrow's pay she would have enough and Stan was not going to get it.

She would think of some way to get rid of Stan, and not lose all her money to him. Angrily wiping away her tears, she went back to work.

Promptly at three Jake entered the library, Katie in tow. Joy was just finishing with a book borrower. "I've got a few more books to put away, then I'll be ready," she told him.

"I'm in no hurry," he said. "I'll just sit here and read while you finish up." Joy returned to her task. She couldn't help comparing Jake to the other men in her life.

Jake is so different than Stan. He always comes at the time he says he will, and he's so patient when I'm not ready. Stan would've come in here yellin' and complainin' that I wasn't ready even if a library customer was still here. Pa, too. He wouldn't ever just sit here. He'd be tellin' me what to do and how to do it, and tellin' me to hurry it up.

Katie wanted to chatter about the new Golden Retriever she'd played with at Mr. Hawkins' house, but Joy spoke sharply to her.

"For heaven's sake, Katie. Must you chatter all the time? Let me finish up here and you can tell me on the way home."

She placed the last book on the shelf, then stood back to admire her work. The new section was bright and cheery. Joy loved color, and had made a display of books with vivid covers to draw the readers' attention to the new sections. *If only life was as simple and colorful as arranging books on a shelf,* she thought.

"It looks great, Joy." Jake had come up behind her and stood close enough to touch, yet he kept his hands to himself and simply admired her work. Joy could sense an electric charge to the atmosphere that hadn't been there a moment before. She moved away.

"Thanks." She was pleased with his compliment. "I'm ready," she said.

Jake looked at her for a moment wishing...then shook his head and smiled. "Well, then let's go. Katie, ready to go?"

"Okay, Mr. Jake. I'll get my coat."

The sleigh pulled up to the farm about four. Gray clouds hung low in the sky but there was plenty of light to see by. "Will we get to build a snowman, Mr. Jake?" Katie asked.

"I reckon we will, that is, if your Momma helps us."

"I should go in and help Ma with supper," Joy said.

"It's early yet, Joy, and this won't take long if all three of us work at it." Jake grinned at her. "Besides, when's the last time you built a snowman?"

"Please, Momma!" Katie jumped up and down in the snow. "Look, we can put it right here by the window."

"Oh, all right, but we'll have to hurry so's I can help Ma." Despite her worries over Stan, Joy just couldn't resist their combined enthusiasm.

"Okay! I'll roll the base, since I'm the biggest," said Jake. "Joy, why don't you roll the middle, and Katie, you can roll the head." They set to work amidst cries of: "This is fun!" "The snow is too cold!" "Wow, this snowball is getting too heavy to push!" It took all three of them to lift the middle section on to the huge base that Jake had rolled. Then Joy and Jake attached the head since Katie was too little to reach.

"I'll get some coal for the eyes and a carrot for the mouth," Katie hollered as she ran for the steps.

"You've done a good job by her, Joy." Jake said, watching Katie run off.

Joy's heart warmed. No one had ever told her that. Stan would tell her she was a bad mother and couldn't do anything right. "She's a good girl. I just hope I do right by her till she's grown," she said, chewing her bottom lip. "Stan always told me I was too easy on her."

Jake felt his stomach clench in anger. There was nothing so far he'd heard about this Stan that showed him any good in the man.

When Katie came out, she trailed a red scarf in one hand, while her other fist clutched a carrot and three pieces of coal. Jake lifted her up so she could insert the coal and carrot into the snowman's face. He tied the scarf around its neck, then rummaged in the sleigh where he found an old hat, which he promptly placed on the snowman's head.

They all stepped back to admire their work. "Wow! It's the biggest and bestest s-s-snowman I ever s-saw," breathed Katie in awe, her teeth chattering with the cold.

"Time to go in, Katie," said her mother. "Run on and get those wet clothes off of you. I'll be right along."

Too cold to argue, Katie headed for the house after first giving Jake a big hug. "Bye. Thank you, Mr. Jake."

"Bye, Katie." He watched the child as she entered the house, then he turned to her mother.

"That was fun, Joy. I think Mr. Snowman looks pretty good, don't you? Course I think my part was the best."

"What?" Joy was indignant. She looked around to see the lumpy snowball she'd first made, then discarded. Picking it up quickly, she threw it at Jake, catching him on the shoulder. "That'll teach you. You know my section is the best."

Some of the snow got under his jacket collar and down his neck. "Oh, so that's how you want to play, is it?" Jake quickly grabbed some snow, and made a fist size snowball. He reached for her as Joy dodged his outstretched arm and ran squealing toward the barn. She tripped over a snowdrift, and Jake caught her as she fell, shoving the snow into her face. They both landed laughing, and scrambled for more snow to ambush each other. Soon the two of them were soaked to the skin.

Finally Joy called "Truce! I'm too cold. We'll have to finish this another day," she said laughing. Her cheeks were bright red from the snow, and her chest rose with each gasp of breath.

Jake was also out of breath. He raised his right arm. "Okay, I surrender. For now, but you've got to admit I won."

"Oh, no. I did." Joy argued. Splat! With a left hook, Jake landed one final snowball on the top of her head.

"Oh, you." She rushed at him with clenched fists to beat on his chest, but Jake easily grasped both of her wrists.

"Sorry, I couldn't waste that last one, could I? Anyway, now I've won for sure, right?"

She looked up at him exhilarated by their war games and by his nearness. Smiling at him through snow covered lashes she melted away all Jake's planned resistance to her charms.

He pulled her to him and planted a tender kiss on her frosty lips, then groaning he thrust her from him and said harshly, "You'd better go in before you catch pneumonia."

Joy touched her lips with her gloved fingers, looked at him in confusion, and then with sinking heart, turned to go. She was almost to the steps when he caught up to her.

"Joy, I'm sorry. I had a great time. Will you still go with me to Pennywhistle on Saturday?"

Nodding her head, Joy murmured "Yes. Thank you for today." She left him there in the snowy yard and quietly entered the house.

Lying awake in bed that night she couldn't help thinking of the two men in her life and contrasting them. Stan, with his devilish smile, who had seemed so much fun when she'd first met him, had turned out to be cruel and cold. Jake, who had looked so intimidating with his unkempt hair and bushy beard had been a gentle giant, showing more love and care for Katie than her own father. Tossing and turning half the night, Joy was determined she would not give in to Stan's demands.

The following day she placed all her pay in an envelope and hid it at the library to retrieve after Stan was gone. She entered the Hungry Bear at exactly four o'clock. Stan was sitting in the back booth. She walked over to him and sat down.

"Well, Babe, you're right on time," he said, gulping down the last of his coffee so fast he slopped it down his chin. "Glad to see you've decided to cooperate." He wiped away the dribble with the back of his hand.

"Stan, you've got to know I don't make much money, and I need it for Katie and me to live on."

He brushed aside her argument with a snarl. "I've got no time for excuses, Joy. I want your pay now. Hand it over if you want the kid left alone."

Joy had saved almost $100.00, and she took it out reluctantly. "Stan, I'll give you all I've saved if you'll go away and promise you'll leave Katie and me alone."

Stan grabbed the envelope. "This is more like it, baby. Sure, I'll leave you alone—for now." He rose and smirked at her. "Until we meet again." With that he left the restaurant, his taunting laugh ringing in her ears.

Chapter Eleven

By Saturday Joe hacked great racking coughs. Worn out after doing his morning chores he took to his bed and stayed there. Consequently he was not present to object when Jake came by for lunch.

Two days of rain had melted away most of the snow. Katie was impatient to see the Christmas decorations, so right after eating they said goodbye to Blanche and set off in Jake's truck. Pennywhistle, a fair size city of about 30,000 people, bustled with early holiday crowds. Multi-colored lights hung across Main Street.

Every department and ten-cent store sported Christmas decorations in their window. The biggest attraction, Lazarus' department store, showed six different Christmas scenes, some of them animated. One exhibit contained a giant train scene with three different trains traveling on separate tracks. Another held a Christmas village with lighted houses.

Figures of people scattered about the toy town looked very realistic, i.e. children riding on a carousel and passengers in horse-drawn carriages. Katie stood a long time in front of this window. "Oh, it looks like a fairyland," she breathed in awe. When they had walked the entire length of Main St. they headed for MacDougal's Eatery where they warmed themselves with hot chocolate.

Joy and Katie were returning to their booth from the Ladies' room when two men lurched out of the adjoining bar. "Well, whatta ya know, if it isn't my ex-missus," came an all too familiar voice.

The little girl had run on ahead, and missed seeing him. Stan's bloodshot eyes watched after her. When Katie reached the booth and slid in beside Jake, Stan glared at Joy, his lips curled in disgust. "So, slut. I see you ain't wasting no time." He held up a hand. "But wait, that's not my business any more. As long as I get my money." He grabbed her sleeve. "I'll expect another installment next week, same time, same place."

"Take your hands off me." Joy spat out the words. "I don't have any more money for you."

"Guess you want to forget you ever had a Katie." He raised his fist to swing at her, then thought better of it when he saw an approaching customer.

Joy, conditioned to shrink when he threatened, found courage in her anger. "You keep your hands off Katie, you hear?"

Deciding to mellow out when he caught Jake looking toward the restrooms, Stan chuckled. "Sure, Babe. For now. But I'll see you on Thursday at the library and I expect the money then, soon's you get paid. Got it?" Giving a hoarse cackle, he shoved her aside and staggered out the door.

She returned to the booth, her face pale, fists clenched at her side. Jake looked up from his conversation with Katie. "Who were you talking to?"

"Oh, just someone I used to know." She couldn't bear to have Jake know that the slovenly drunk was the man she had married.

The rest of the afternoon was spent at the movies, watching a double feature. Joy stayed distracted, consumed with dread, trying to think of a way to protect Katie and get Stan out of her life.

Jake noticed her tension on the drive home as she sat quietly, her thoughts far away, alternately twisting her hands and clenching her fists. When they pulled into the farmyard, Katie ran into the house to tell her grandparents about her day. Jake turned to Joy. "Well, are you going to tell me what's bothering you?"

"N'nothin'."

"Don't try to fool me, Joy!" He gently grasped her shoulders, gazing intently into her eyes. "You're talkin' to Jake here, and I want to help." Tenderly he massaged her shoulders and upper arms, releasing some of the tension. Joy burst into tears.

"N'no one can help. I've got to figure it out by myself. He's not going to hurt Katie," she wailed.

Jake held her close while she sobbed out her fear and frustration, then he pulled out a handkerchief and gently wiped away her tears. "Hey, hey, what's this?" He thrust her away from him in order to give her his full attention, while continuing to hold her hand.

"Now, what's this all about? Believe me, no one is going to hurt Katie. Why, that little tyke wouldn't harm a fly. Where would she get an enemy who'd want to bother her?"

"It's Stan, Katie's Daddy. He wants me to pay him money every week. If I don't, he says he'll take her away and I'll never see her again."

Jake, who'd grown to love Katie as if she were his own child, slammed his hand on the steering wheel. "Where's he staying? I'll see that he leaves you alone."

"I don't know where he stays. He just came to the library the other day."

Joy wouldn't tell him that Stan planned to return to the library on Thursday. She just couldn't be obliged to him again. She opened the car door and stepped out.

"There's nothing you can do, Jake. This is between Stan and me. I'll just have to figure something out."

"Fine, if that's what you want. Don't trust me. Don't trust anyone. Miss Joy can do it all herself." He put the car in reverse, wheeled around, and sped away, unwilling to let Joy see his hurt. She stood staring after him in dismay.

"It's between Stan and me, she says. "Wal, far be it from me to interfere in Miss Joy's life," Jake muttered as he headed back home.

Jake avoided Joy all week. She missed him, but couldn't bring herself to think of any way to apologize. She needed all her energy to plan a way to defeat Stan and be rid of him. Besides, she was sure she was right. It wasn't Jake's business. Hadn't her folks taught her to keep her affairs to herself? Even Stan had preached this philosophy.

"Momma, why doesn't Mr. Jake come to see us anymore?" Katie grilled her at least twice daily.

Her answers were monotonous in their repetition. "I don't know, Katie. He's probably busy with his chores on the farm." She dreaded Thursday when she would have to face up to Stan, but events intervened to postpone that confrontation.

Monday morning while Joy was eating her breakfast, Blanche rushed into the kitchen. A worn bathrobe wrapped loosely around her old flannel nightgown, hair uncombed, the braid coming apart, a panicked expression on her face.

"Joy, I need your help. Will you take care of feedin' the animals and then go for the doctor? Pa's burning up, and talkin' out of his head." She wiped her straggly hair out of her eyes and pulled a shawl over her bathrobe, shivering in the unheated kitchen.

Sinking down on a wooden chair, she put her head in her hands. "He's been up all night coughin'."

Joy poured her mother a cup of tea. "Sit here and rest for a bit. I'll be right back." She grabbed a jacket off the hook in the entry and ran to feed the animals, then returned to the kitchen to wash up and take her leave. Noting the black circles framing Blanche's red-rimmed eyes, she decided to stop by the library and ask for the day off. Twenty minutes later she pulled up at the home of the local doctor. Rousing Dr. Clement from his second cup of coffee, she filled him in on the course of her Pa's illness as far as she knew it, then hurried to the library.

"Miss O'Brien, Ma needs me. Pa's sick, and she's not lookin' too good herself right now."

"Of course, child. You take as much time as you need. Just let me know how things are going when you can. Don't worry about your job. It'll be waiting for you."

"How is he?" Blanche asked as the doctor softly closed the door to Joe's room. Dr. Clement shook his head as he put the stethoscope back into his bag.

"He's about as sick as a man can be. I've given him something to calm that cough and help him sleep, but the next twenty-four hours are critical. You've got to get that fever down somehow. I suggest you bathe him in lukewarm water every hour. I'll check back on him in the morning."

"What is it, Doctor?" Joy asked.

"His lungs are filled up with fluid. I'd say he's got a bad case of pneumonia."

"Is he goin' to be all right?"

"Can't rightly tell. You just do as I say, and we'll see how he is tomorrow." He took his hat and coat down off the hook. "I'll let myself out. See you in the morning."

Joy and Blanche immediately began preparing water for bathing Joe, and took turns throughout the day placing lukewarm cloths on him. They checked his temperature frequently, but it seemed as if it would only go down a degree after intense sponging, stay down briefly and shoot up again.

Katie wandered about the house clinging to her kittens, and looking like a lost urchin. She worried about her grandfather, but her Momma and Grammy were too busy to pay her any attention. At last she pulled on her coat and went out to visit the animals.

"I don't know if my Grampa is going to die," she told the horse as she fed him a carrot. "I'm skeered, Buttons." The horse nuzzled his head against her cheek as if to comfort her and Katie burst into tears.

Inside, Blanche wearily squeezed out yet another lukewarm cloth and laid it on Joe's forehead.

"Ma, you look worn out. Why don't you go fix us a quick bite to eat and I'll finish up here," Joy said.

Blanche rubbed the tendrils of hair off her forehead and straightened up. "Okay, I'd better feed that young'un, too. Poor thing ain't had much attention today."

Jake wanted to help Joy, but she was so damn stubborn. He stayed away from her to sort out his thoughts. Somehow he had to convince her he wasn't anything like the man she had married.

Mulling over all he knew about Stan, he was convinced he'd get nowhere with her until Stan was out of the picture. She'd be spending all her energy trying to outwit the man. From what he could tell, this would get her nowhere.

He'd known men before with the kind of vicious nature this man had. They were snakes who took advantage of the weak and innocent, cowards who liked the feeling of power they got from intimidating women and children. And once they thought they had a good thing going, they'd hang on to grab all they could from it. He'd have to find this guy and have a talk with him whether Joy liked it or not.

He checked around town with the help of Sheriff Luke Falkner, a friend of his, but Stan wasn't registered in the local motels or flophouses. So Jake began staking out the library in the afternoons, whenever he could break away from farm chores, hoping to catch Stan the next time he approached Joy. He alternated his time in town between the library, his car, and the café across the street from the library, where he had a good view of the front door. There was no sign of Stan all week, and he wondered whether his plan to catch him was a dumb idea.

Joy hadn't been in all week, and he worried about her. But since he'd had coffee one morning with the doc, he now knew she was home taking care of her Pa.

Joe's temperature climbed steadily on Wednesday night. It registered 104 degrees about ten o'clock. Blanche and Joy had to take turns holding him down in order for the other one to bathe him or spoon broth and water into him. He was so out of his head that he thrashed about the bed, knocking over the mist tent they had built around him, and yelling out to his Ma and Pa.

"Don't hit her, Pa. She didn't do anything," he screamed. "Okay, okay, you can hit me. It's all right, Ma. I can take it, just so's he leaves you alone."

Joy and Blanche stared across the bed at each other.

"What is it, Ma? Why is he sayin' that?"

"I dunno. I think he's rememberin' about his childhood."

"Did his Pa beat him?"

Suddenly Joe began screaming in a high-pitched wail, sounding like a small boy. "No, Pa!"

Chapter Twelve

"Hush Joe, hush. It's okay. I'm here, me and Joy," Blanche said, rubbing her hands on his shoulders as she firmly but gently pushed him back down on his pillow. She pulled the covers around him and looked up at Joy.

"I dunno, Joy. He never would talk about his Pa, just said he was dead and buried and good riddance. His Ma was dead too when I met him, but Pa seemed to have some feelin' for her though he never would talk much about her, either." Blanche sank down on the chair they'd brought up from the kitchen, and buried her face in her hands. Her shoulders quivered as she silently gave in to the fears that tugged at her.

Joy took a deep breath and reached out to rub her hand over her Ma's neck and shoulders. "It'll be okay, Ma."

Blanche swallowed. Choking back her sobs, she squeezed hard on Joy's hand until it hurt. "Yeah. I'm glad you're here, Joy."

Joe's wails began to get louder, and Joy spoke softly to him. "Pa, it's me, Joy. It's all right now. Here, take some of this water." She spooned some of the cool drink between his parched lips.

Suddenly Joe sat up straight and looked right at her. "I'm sorry, Joy. I never knew how to be a Pa." He fell back against the covers, his eyes closed and his breath slowed to an even pace. They watched him as the thrashing subsided and he lay still.

"I think he'll sleep, now," Blanche said. "You go on to bed, Joy. I'll lay down here on these blankets on the floor."

Joy tiptoed into the room she shared with Katie and stood looking down at her child. She bit her lower lip. Tears threatened to spill onto her cheeks as she thought of what her Pa must have gone through when he wasn't any older than Katie. She undressed slowly, put on a nightgown, then sat by the window staring out at the darkness.

A half moon shone down pale light onto the barn and outbuildings. She thought of how her Pa must have had to start out with nothing, his own Pa so mean. He'd built a comfortable spread, just him and Ma. She knew he'd worked hard all his life for this. It was Pa who'd kept it all going in hard times, she knew, working the farm mostly by himself the years Ma worked in the store.

She thought of what he'd said to her and if he'd remember when he got well. *If* he got well. And what she'd say to him. She wondered what her life would have been like if her and Pa had got along better. And how much their problems with each other were caused by the unknown grandparents.

Where do we go from here, she wondered knowing things would never be the same. She couldn't ever look at her Pa again as just a mean, unloving man. There were reasons for him acting the way he did. 'Course that didn't make it right, she knew. He'd sure treated her rotten all them years. Still, look what good come from it. If she hadn't been driven away, she'd never have had Katie. She smiled at the sleeping child and thanked God for this gift.

Slipping under the covers, she gently moved Katie over closer to the wall. Joy's last thoughts before falling into a weary sleep were *Stan's not going to get Katie.*

On Thursday Jake was sitting in a corner of the library flipping through magazines, when he heard a shout near the front door and the pounding of a fist on the librarian's desk.

"What do you mean she's not here? She was supposed to meet me today. She's got something of mine and she'd better cough it up." Stan lurched drunkenly across the counter, shaking his fist. "Now where is she?"

Miss O'Brien cringed behind her desk and sat down quickly. "I-I don't know, but she's not here. This is a library, and you m-must keep the noise down."

"It'll be a cold day in hell when you or any woman tells me what to do," Stan threatened, then spun around as he felt a strong grip on his shoulder. Jake had leaped to his feet at the first sign of disturbance and now had him by the collar.

"I think you owe the lady an apology," he said.

"No way in hell," Stan replied, twisting to free himself. But Jake put a stranglehold on Stan's neck, effectively cutting off the circulation.

"I guess you'd better rethink that, Mister." He loosened his grip slightly. "Now what do you say to the lady?"

Gasping for air, Stan blurted, "Sorry," while glaring at Jake and trying to get into position to punch him. Instead, he found himself thrust forward out the door onto the street where Jake flung him like a shovelful of dirt. He sprang to his feet and came at Jake with head lowered and tried to butt him in the stomach. Jake was ready for him and repelled him with a blow to his right temple.

Stan was no match for Jake in a fair fight, but Stan didn't believe in fighting fair. He pulled a few surprises, hitting Jake below the belt and almost having him down for the count before Jake knocked him backward with a right hook.

A small crowd had gathered, the women crying out in horror and the men making bets. Suddenly the sheriff appeared. "All right, folks, break it up. Now what happened here?" he asked.

"This man assaulted me," Stan blubbered.

"Is that right?" The sheriff looked at Jake in disbelief. "I've never known Jake here to attack anyone. Why don't we go over to the station while we sort this out."

Jake dusted himself off. "Sure thing, Luke."

Stan looked at them, suddenly sober. "Nah," he said. "Let's drop it. I guess I won't press charges."

"What about you, Jake?" asked the sheriff. "Do you want to drop it?"

"You may want to know what he was doing in the library threatening Miss O'Brien, Sheriff. I believe he's made threats against Joy Russell, too. This here is Stan Bender, the guy that run out on her and her little girl."

"Is that right? Well, young man, it seems you'd better come over to the station after all." The sheriff nodded to the bystanders. "Okay, folks. You can go about your business, now." At the station house, Sheriff Luke listened to both Jake and Stan's stories, then booked Stan for being drunk, disorderly and disturbing the peace. "I guess it won't do any harm to let you cool down a bit and sleep it off," he said. "Jake, you'd better get on home and put something on that eye. Looks like you're going to have quite a shiner there."

"Yeah, Luke, I'm going. But I want you to know," Jake said to Stan, "when the sheriff lets you out of here, you'd better get out of town. And don't come around here again. You touch one hair on Joy or Katie, and I'll come after you myself."

* * *

On Friday Joe's fever rose again and he coughed in spasms all day. The doctor looked in about noon, increased his sulfa prescription and showed them how to make mustard plasters to draw out the congestion. When they weren't sitting with Joe, Joy and Blanche took turns lying on the couch, trying to get some rest.

Joy took over the care of her Pa for the first part of that night, urging an exhausted Blanche to get a good night's sleep, promising to wake her Ma about five. She bundled up in blankets on the floor beside Joe's bed, while Blanche slept in her room with Katie. "Call me if there's any change," Blanche had said.

"I will, Ma."

Blanche felt like a quitter leaving Joe, but knew Joy was right in pushing her to get some rest. She couldn't be any good to him if she got sick herself, and right now she was so tired she could hardly make it to the next room for the dizziness that swept over her. She was asleep five minutes after her head touched the pillow.

About one, Joe began calling out and thrashing around in the bed. Joy jumped up from the floor where she'd been dozing, and went to him. "What is it, Pa?"

He sat up and swung his legs over the side. "Got to pee," he said, trying to get up.

"Wait, Pa." Joy handed him a milk bottle to use. "I'll be right outside till you're finished," she said. When Joe was done, he lay back against the pillows. He could feel the sweat running down his neck and back and he knew the fever had broken. He lay there thinking of Joy and Blanche. They had been at his side, one or the other, every time he woke, day or night. He knew he'd been pretty sick and he dimly remembered dreams of his Ma and Pa. He thought back on his life with Blanche and how he'd acted just like his Pa when he'd beat on Blanche and Joy. He didn't deserve them takin' such good care of him when he was so sick.

"Joy, come on in here," he called. She walked back into the room and over to the bed.

"You seem a little better, Pa." She rubbed his back a bit. He seemed clearer in his head and wanting to talk, so she sat by his bed in the straight back chair they'd brought up from the kitchen.

"What did I say when I was out of it?" he asked her.

"Well, Pa, you was shoutin'."

"What was I shoutin'?"

"Somethin' about, 'don't hit me.' I think you thought you was talkin' to your Pa." Joy looked down at the floor. "Did he hit you much, Pa?"

Joe sat up and grabbed his pillow. "Joy, I'm gonna tell you how it was between my Pa and Ma and me." He punched the pillow and stuffed it behind his head. "I think it's time you knew, so you won't ever get yourself and Katie in the same kind of trouble we had."

"What do you mean, Pa?"

Joe cleared his throat, swallowed a sip of water from a glass on his bedside table, and began to speak. "I was five when Pa lost his job the first time. That's when the drinkin' started."

"Did he drink a lot?"

"Yeah. He drank a lot." Joe looked at Joy in the dim lamplight and smiled sadly. "A lot. Just like your own Pa did." He pulled at his covers, scrunching them into a ball in his hand. "When he couldn't find a beer, that's when the beatings began. He'd yell at Ma and say she had hid 'em. Then he'd…" Joe's voice broke and he pulled again at his blanket, twisting it tightly.

"It's all right, Pa. You don't have to tell me." Joy sat fighting back tears as she thought of the little boy her Pa had been and the pain he'd had.

But Joe wouldn't be put off. "Yes, gal. I do have to tell you. And I want you to hear me, so's you understand how it was. Pa would grab a switch or his belt…" He clenched his fists, his thoughts of the past causing his stomach to tighten up in knots.

"He'd say, 'I'm gonna teach you to count, boy.' Then…then he'd make Ma turn her back to him and he'd count up to ten or fifteen or twenty." Joe shut his eyes, squeezing them tight to fight back threatening tears. "Then he'd whip her with each number he'd say."

"Oh, Pa." Joy lost the fight she was having with her tears and they ran out of the corners of her eyes. "Why are you tellin' me this?"

"I guess cause I'm tryin' to understand it, myself. I remember how I hated him, and how I promised myself I'd get away from all that someday."

"You did, Pa. You married Ma when you was real young, didn't you?"

"Yeah. Only I brought it all with me. Well, maybe I didn't beat on your Ma too much. All right, I guess I did, when we was young, 'specially when I was makin' my own brew. But I shouldn'ta done it even once. Then there was that time I slammed you against the wall."

Joe gazed at Joy, his tears sliding down his cheeks and dropping on to his flannels. "I've been a lousy Pa to ya." He reached out his hand and patted her arm. "I've been tellin' ya all this 'cause I'm sorry and I want you to know that."

"Oh, Pa." Joy buried her head on his outstretched arm and sobbed. He pulled her close and hugged her.

Chapter Thirteen

In the morning, Joe's skin was much cooler to the touch. He'd slept four or five hours and felt a little hungry. When he opened his eyes, he saw Blanche sleeping on the floor and he called out. "What are ya doing down there Blanche? You'll get pneumonia layin' on the floor!"

Blanche jumped up and felt his forehead. "Joe! You're better! I was so worried."

"No need to worry 'bout me, woman. Can't get rid of me that easy. Now what's to eat? Feel like I ain't ate fer a week."

"I'll fix you some hot cereal and bring it up right away. You rest now, y'hear?"

Blanche hurried downstairs to the kitchen, where Joy was just coming in from tending the animals. "Joy, your Pa's better! He's even askin' for food. He's going to get well." Her lips trembled, and she sat down quickly, wiping her eyes with a dishtowel.

"I know, Ma." Joy shed her coat and huddled over the stove to warm up. "The fever broke in the night. I'll fix his breakfast if you want to take him some fresh water to wash up."

Moments later Blanche set the wash things down by Joe's bed. "Joy's bringin' up your breakfast." She handed him the dampened wash cloth. "You've been mighty sick, Joe."

He looked at her in some embarrassment. "Yeah. I guess I gave you all a hard time, huh?"

"Well, you was pretty much out of it. We had to hold your arms still when you was thrashing around from the fever."

Joe sponged his face and hands with the warm water. "This sure feels good," he said.

Just then Joy brought a tray of oatmeal and a piece of toast. "Here you are, Pa." Blanche cleared away the wash things and started for the door.

"I'll take those downstairs, Ma," Joy said. "Since Pa's better, guess I'd better get back in to work at the library. I'll see you later, Pa."

Blanche sat by the bed while Joe ate. Her eyes closed, she rested, weary to the bone.

"You look mighty wore down, Blanche," Joe said, finishing up his meal. "How long have I been out of it? A couple days?"

"Oh, more than that. You took to your bed on Monday."

"What day's today?"

"Saturday."

"Oh." Joe's eyes opened wide. "Who's been takin' care of the animals and the chores?"

"Joy and me. And even Katie helped some."

Joe was uncomfortable. He was used to taking care of things himself and not owing anybody if he could help it. "Well, I thanks ya." He reached out and squeezed Blanche's hand. At his unexpected tenderness, Blanche dropped her head on the bed and sobbed. "I thought we was going to lose you," she said.

"Hey, now." He ran his hands through her hair. "I told you ya can't get rid of me that easy. Seems to me you need some rest yourself. I'm gonna come downstairs and sit in the livin' room. Maybe you can lie down on the couch and we'll both watch Katie today. Where is my granddaughter anyway?"

"I'm right here, Grampa." Katie stood shyly in the doorway, where she'd stopped when she saw her Grammy crying. "Are you all better?"

"Not all better yet, Katie, but I 'spect I'm on the mend. I'll just have to rest a lot till I get my strength back, I guess."

"I'll help you, Grampa. I'll visit you like you was in the hospital, and I'll bring the kittens to visit and we can read books and…"

"Hold it, Katie. Why don't we take it a little at a time? When I'm stronger we can do all that. These first couple of days, I think I'll still be sleepin' a lot. How are the kittens, by the way?"

"Oh, Grampa, they play all the time. They took Grammy's ball o' yarn and chased it around the room. They like to chase each other's tails, too."

"Have you named them yet?"

Katie looked down at her feet. "Yeah. One is Jo-Jo. I named him for you. And the girl is Beejay for Grammy and Momma."

"Let me see. B for Blanche and J for Joy, is that it?"

"Yeah, Grampa, how did you guess?"

Joe smiled down at her. "Grampa's are just smart, I guess. Now go git your breakfast while I put m'clothes on."

After Blanche and Katie went down to the kitchen, Joe pulled on a pair of pants and flannel shirt, then fell back on the bed, winded from the exertion. "Guess I'm not as strong as I thought I was," he said to himself. He decided to rest a bit longer before trying to make it downstairs.

While he lay waiting for Blanche to return to help him, he thought back on what he remembered of his illness. He had memories of Blanche's worried face hovering over him, of her scooping broth to his lips, and spoonfuls of water. He knew she had bathed him continually, and he vaguely remembered lashing out at her. Thoughts of her faithfulness in spite of his hot temper and nastiness to her over the years made him ashamed.

He thought too of Joy and the way he had treated her, and still she'd helped feed and bathe him while he was sick. When it came right down to it he hadn't treated his family any better than his Pa had treated him and his Ma. In the end his Ma had run off with another man, saying she couldn't take it any longer. He couldn't blame her. She'd put up with his Pa's beatings for eighteen years, till Joe was grown and out on his own. He was luckier than his Pa. Blanche and Joy hadn't given up on him yet. They were still with him. Well, maybe he'd better mend his fences before it was too late.

It was mid-morning before Joy got to work. The library was crowded with children out of school for a holiday weekend and Miss O'Brien was very busy helping them find books while trying to keep the little ones quiet.

"Oh, Joy, I'm so glad you're here. How's your Pa?" She didn't wait for an answer. "Why don't you take these young ones over to the children's corner and read them a story, while I find some of the reference books these sixth graders are looking for."

It wasn't until Joy was leaving at 2:00, that Miss O'Brien mentioned Stan's visit. "There was a man here looking for you the other day. He said you had something of his, and he was very angry that you weren't here. In fact he became quite threatening."

"Oh, Miss O'Brien, I'm sorry. He shouldna' bothered you." Joy looked at the floor. "I'll tell him he can't come back here."

"I don't think he'll be back. Jake Jorgensen was here, and he made him apologize to me and leave. I guess they got into a scuffle outside."

"Did anyone get hurt?"

"I don't know too much about it. I stayed in so I didn't see what happened." She stamped some returned books with the date, and set them aside. "Sheriff Falkner locked up the other man overnight. I heard he released him the next morning and ran him out of town. Told him he's not welcome here and not to come back."

This was good news to Joy, although she wasn't sure Stan would stay away as ordered. She wondered what Jake had been doing at the library at just the right time to help. She decided to drive by his place before going home and thank him for stopping Stan. This was her excuse, anyway. What she really wanted was to see for herself that he wasn't hurt.

When she pulled into his yard, she sat for a moment gathering her courage. She remembered the last time she'd seen him, when she'd told him she'd have to solve her problem with Stan by herself. He'd been really mad when he'd left her. And he hadn't been around since. Maybe he didn't want to have anything more to do with her. Well, she still owed him a thank you. She walked slowly to his side porch and knocked on the door. When he didn't answer right away, she turned to go, thinking he either wasn't home or he didn't want to see her. Suddenly the door was flung open wide, and Jake stood there with the purplest eye she'd ever seen.

Joy gasped. "Oh, Jake, what did he do to you? Are you all right?"

"Well, if it isn't Miss Joy," Jake said, his smile grim. "The Independent Girl Wonder who fixes everything herself." He stepped aside. "You might as well come in. And what brings you out here?"

Joy followed him into his kitchen. "I-I wanted to thank you for what you did the other day with Stan. He really scared Miss O'Brien. And I don't know what would have happened if you hadn't been there."

"Me?" Jake said. "I didn't do much, just got him out of there so he wouldn't bother her. Sheriff Falkner's the one who locked him up."

"You must have done more than that. Look at your eye. And I know how violent Stan gets when he's drinking. Specially if he wants somethin'."

"Wal, it's over now, and he'll think twice about starting trouble in this town again. The sheriff told him he's giving him this one chance. If he comes back he'll be thrown in jail." Jake poured two mugs of tea, and set them on the table. "The way Luke tells it, he told him he'll lock him up and throw away the key." He passed her the sugar. "Now how are you getting along? Taking care of everything yourself, are you?"

Joy wilted. Jake was still mad at her for not letting him help, and she didn't understand why it was so important to him. "Jake, I'm sorry I made you mad the other day. I didn't mean to."

Jake ran his hands through his hair. "What can I say, Joy? I know you've been through some tough times and have had to do for yourself. But you've got to let others help sometimes. You've got to learn to trust. That's what being friends is all about."

Joy stirred sugar into her tea. "It isn't that I don't trust you. It's just that I-I..."

"I know. You've got to do it yourself. Well, until you can trust me I don't see our friendship going anywhere."

Joy stood up, her sadness visible on her face. "I guess if you don't want to be friends that's okay with me, Mr. Jake."

It was all Jake could do not to take her in his arms and kiss away the hurt. Instead, he said, "Joy, it's not what I want, but I can't go on this way. I'll still look in on you and Katie from time to time. If you need anything, I'm hoping you'll let me know. I'm here for you, but you're going to have to show me you trust me before we can have a real relationship."

"I don't know what more you want," Joy said. "I trust you every time I get in a car with you, every time we go anywhere together." She turned to leave. "I've got to go home." It was too much, all that worry about Stan and Pa, and now Jake. She just wanted to get away before she made a fool of herself and sobbed her heart out in front of him.

Jake strode around the table, catching her before she got out the door. He gently turned her around and ever so gently kissed her. His lips grazed hers while he pulled her into a tender embrace. Joy wanted to put her head on his shoulder and bawl, but her pride wouldn't let her. She drew back and stared up at him. "Goodbye, Jake." Pushing open the kitchen door she ran down the steps fighting her tears.

Jake stood on the porch watching her go. "Think on what I said, Joy. Please," he said. He watched as she turned the car around and headed out to the road, then he kicked open the door and went inside slamming it behind him.

Joe leaned on Blanche as he made his way downstairs. He sat on the couch in the living room. She propped him with pillows and covered him with a blanket, then sat at the other end of the sofa with her knitting. Katie had gone outside to play with her kittens and they were alone. Joe cleared his throat. "Blanche?"

"Yeah?"

"You've stuck around me a long time."

"Where else would I be? You was sick."

"No, I mean all these years."

"Yeah."

"Why'd ya hang around? I didn't treat you very good."

Blanche stared at him in surprise. So far as she knew he'd never owned up he was at fault before. "I dunno. Guess I was hopin'…"

"What was you hopin', Blanche?"

"Maybe that you'd change, I guess."

"You've waited a long time for that."

"Yeah."

"I'm gonna need your help." He smiled at her.

She couldn't remember when she'd last seen him smile like that. Not since before the hard times, she guessed. She looked at him hopefully. "How, Joe?"

"I've been doin' a lot of thinkin'. And I'm gonna try and make it up to you. But sometimes I might forget and lose my temper like before. Just be patient with me, okay?"

"Oh, Joe."

"Come over here by me." She moved to his end of the sofa and Joe put his arm around her. "Thanks for takin' such good care of me when I was sick," he said.

Blanche put her head on his chest. "Tweren't nothin'," she said and closed her eyes.

Chapter Fourteen

The snow started two weeks before Christmas. For several days the flakes fell until at least four feet of snow covered the ground. Schools and the library were closed, and roads were left unplowed. The temperature dropped to twelve below and the wind howled relentlessly. This caused huge drifts so the town decided to wait until the wind quit before attempting to clear the roads.

Blanche cooked pots of hot soups to help keep them warm and Joy experimented with baking bread. Katie and Joe played checkers by the hour and she entertained him with little stories she made up each day. The child had a vivid imagination.

Blanche and Joy also worked on knitting projects, and Joy taught Katie how to do some needlework with leftover yarn. Joe took up his whittling again, but set it aside whenever Katie appeared. He was making some doll figures for her for Christmas and didn't want to spoil the surprise. It was a cozy time for them, Joy thought, probably the homiest time she could remember. It would have been perfect if only Jake were there too. Pa hadn't lost his temper but once since he'd come downstairs after being sick.

He'd even told her he was sorry about that time he'd called her a slut and slapped her. She didn't know what to make of it. He and Ma seemed so much closer somehow. It brought back vague memories of a time that she barely remembered, when she was a very little girl, before the bad times hit.

Oh, but she missed Jake. She'd cried herself to sleep every night for a week after she'd left him that day. She now knew how hard he'd fought Stan to help her. Sheriff Luke had told her how Jake had gone to the library every day to protect her if Stan showed up. The sheriff knew that Stan had threatened to take Katie, too, and had warned her that this would be a kidnapping if it happened, which meant that the law would become involved.

He also said he'd hire Jake in a minute if he needed extra help. He said Jake was the most trustworthy man he knew. She mulled over that and all that Jake had said to her that day, confused because she'd always felt it was her responsibility to protect Katie. And to take care of them both. How could she be lookin' to Jake to take care of them?

She was heading for the barn with Katie one afternoon just before supper when she saw that their two horses had gotten out of the pasture. They were across the road nudging the now melting snow looking for grass beneath to graze on. "Katie, you stay here, while I bring them back," she said. "You can feed the chickens while I'm gone."

"Okay, Momma." Katie gossiped to the chickens who had been moved inside the barn for warmth. "Come on, girls. Here's your supper."

Suddenly a hand was clamped over her mouth, and before she could see who had her, she heard the voice she dreaded most in all the world, her Daddy. "Not one sound, when I let you go, Katie," he snarled. "Hear me?" She nodded fearfully.

"Good. We understand each other." He released her. "Now I want you to come with me. We're just gonna play a little trick on your Momma." He snickered hoarsely and she could smell his whiskey breath.

"I don't want to go," she whimpered, and felt the crack of his hand on the side of her head. He yanked her by the arm. "Come on now, not another word, ya hear?" Katie's eyes were glazed with shock. She nodded again, tears streaming silently down her face.

"We're goin' for a little ride," said Stan, cackling again. He pulled her out the side door and around to the back of the barn, where he had horses waiting with a grizzly man Katie had never seen before. "This here's Hank. Hank, this here's my daughter," he said. "Up you go, Katie." He lifted her up on to the back of his horse and a moment later they were headed across the fields.

Joy, in the meantime, struggled with the horses. "Come on, Buttons, if you come, Sandy will too," she said as she tugged at their collars. Finally she remembered the carrots in her pocket and held them out. With a whinny, Buttons tossed his head and began moving slowly toward her. Joy retreated step by step, leading him into the pasture, Sandy following after.

"I don't know how that gate got open," she said to herself, puzzled. "I'm sure it was latched." Once the horses trotted safely back inside, she hooked the gate and returned to the barn.

"Okay, Katie, I'm back. Are the chickens all fed? I'm cold. Let's go inside." Utter silence. Joy looked around the barn. "Katie, where are you? Come on. This isn't the time to play hide and seek. It's too cold out here." Still no answer. Joy became impatient. "Katie, I said come out right now." She began searching the horse stalls. "Katie, Katie!" Deciding Katie must have gone back into the house, she headed for the steps. She kicked off the snow in the entry and started to remove her coat.

"Where's Katie?" Blanche asked from her place by the stove. "I've got supper almost ready, just in time to warm her up."

Joy's mouth dropped open. "Ma, didn't she come in here?"

Alarmed, Blanche shook her head. "No, I've been right here all the time. I'd have seen her if she came in."

"I'll be right back, Ma." Joy ran outside, her coat half on and half off. The cold was bitter with the wind still gusting at times, and she buttoned up as she ran. She raced to the barn, calling "Katie, Katie."

She searched through every stall again, then rushed outside to look in the chicken house and other outbuildings. There was no sign of her daughter. Slowing down to catch her breath, Joy began to look in the snow for footprints, realizing she'd probably covered them up with her scurrying. She returned to the barn for one last look and to her surprise she found a note nailed to the side door.

Joy, you'd better get five hundred dollars to me by tomorrow at 3:00 PM. I'll look for it at our old hiding place. Put the money there and I'll leave a note where you can find Katie. Don't tell anyone if you want Katie back.

Joy rushed outside and found fresh hoof prints, and small footprints that must surely be Katie's. When she saw a man's large footprints next to them her hand went to her mouth and she screamed. "No, oh, Katie! Noooo!" She ran across the field trying to follow the trail, but knew she'd never catch up.

"Joy, Joy, have you found her?" Her Ma was shouting from the doorway as she clumped through the drifts back to the house.

"No, Ma, Stan's taken her," Joy wailed as she reached the entry. She stomped the snow off her boots and entered the kitchen.

Joe called out from the living room. "What's this you say, Joy? He'd better not harm a hair on that girl's head or he'll answer to me." He came into the kitchen and grabbed his coat from the entry.

"Where are you going, Joe?" Blanche screamed. "You're not over your pneumonia. Do you want to get sick all over again?"

"Someone's got to go after that little girl," he said.

"Pa, you're not strong enough yet. Stay here. I-I'll go get Jake. He'll help, and someone's got to be here if they come back," Joy said. "Pa, I'll get help, I promise."

She left the house, warmed up her car engine then slowly drove to Jake's, cursing the snow that delayed her. Pulling up to his house, she flung open the car door and sprinted up the cleared driveway.

"Jake, Jake," she hollered, crying and banging on the door. Jake threw it open, took one look at her and pulled her into his arms.

"What's the matter, Joy, what's happened?" He held her close while she sobbed out her story.

"Stan's come back. He's got Katie. He took her from the barn just now. We've got to find them."

"What in hell does he think he's doing?" Jake's fist slammed the wall. He grabbed his coat. "Let's go.

"Where are we going?"

"To report it to the sheriff. I don't suppose you've done that, yet?"

"N-no, I came right here."

He led her to his truck. "This'll do better in the snow. Now tell me the rest."

"He left a note and he wants five hundred dollars by tomorrow. I don't have that much money," she wailed. "He says I'll never see her again if I tell anybody." She looked at him in horror. "Oh, Jake, don't let on that you know anything. He'll hurt Katie, I know he will. And I can't tell the sheriff."

"Joy, you did right to tell me and we've got to tell the sheriff. It's his job and he's good at it. Don't you see? You don't have to figure this out by yourself. Don't worry. We'll find him for you." He squeezed her hand. "We'll get her back, somehow, Joy. I promise you." *And she'd better be unhurt or Stan won't know what hit him,* he vowed silently.

Sheriff Luke, furious when he learned of the abduction, couldn't wait to get his hands on Stan again. "That no account... I should have locked him up and thrown away the key when I had the chance. Don't worry, Joy. If we don't find him before the drop-off time tomorrow, we'll get the money together somehow. Now tell me everything you know."

She told him what she could. The sheriff asked where the drop-off place was that Stan had mentioned in the note. At first she refused to tell him that. "I don't want any one but me to go there.

If Stan sees anyone else, he may not give Katie back."

"Joy, you've got to trust Sheriff Luke," said Jake. "He knows his job, and he's not going to let Stan see him."

"We'll stake out the place early and keep low till after you've got Katie back, Joy," said Luke. "Now what do you say?"

Joy looked at Jake. Her heart leaped at his reassuring smile and she thought, *well, I haven't done such a good job of protecting Katie by myself. I guess it's time I tried some of this trust Jake is always talking about.*

"All right," she said. "We used to leave messages for each other in a hollowed out oak down by the river."

"We'll check it out, but first let's go out to your place," Sheriff Luke said. "I want to take a look at those prints before dark."

After checking with Blanche and learning Katie had not come back, they searched the barn again for evidence, but found nothing except some spilled corn dropped by Katie when she'd been grabbed. The sheriff retrieved Stan's note from the nail and went out back to study the prints. Since it was almost dark he decided it was too late to follow them.

"I'll be here first thing in the morning, Joy, with horses and a couple of deputies. Now can you show me that tree? I want to get a feel for the place before tomorrow and plan where to hide my men."

At the river Joy showed them the spot which once had been the substance of her dreams, and now was the focus of her nightmare. She shuddered when she looked at the tree. "It's right in here where he wants the money," she said, showing them a hollowed out area in the Y of two branches. They cleared away the snow and found it half full of acorns, stuffed away by squirrels for the winter.

"Don't you worry, Joy," said Sheriff Luke. "We're going to get him. He's not going to get away with this."

"I'll be there tomorrow, too, Luke. You can count on me," Jake said. He turned to Joy. "She'll be all right tonight. You know he's not going to hurt her before three o'clock tomorrow. Not when she's his ticket to five hundred dollars."

"We'll get some men and ride their trail in the morning," said the sheriff. "And if we don't catch up to them we know he'll be at the river for his money by three. We'll get him then." Although frantic with worry, Joy knew there was nothing more they could do until daylight. It was already getting too dark to see the end of her finger. The sheriff dropped them off at Joy's place, and Jake held her tightly for a moment before saying goodnight. She absorbed some of his strength as she nestled against him.

"I'll be here first thing in the morning, Joy. Try not to worry, and get some sleep." He kissed her gently and left.

Katie shivered. She lay on a dirty-smelling cot in the loft of an old shack her Daddy had said belonged to his friend, Hank. The two men sat by the fire down below her, drinking and playing cards. They slurred their speech, but she could make out a few words every now and then. She knew that Stan would hit her if she made any noise and she bit her lip to keep from crying out.

Chill drafts eased their way in from the roof, and despite the fire down below, she was cold. Hungry, too. She'd missed her supper, and her Daddy'd only given her a piece of stale bread when they'd got to the cabin. She wondered if she'd ever see her Momma again. She held herself rigid against the sour smelling bed but finally, worn out from fear and worry, she curled into a little ball and fell asleep.

In the morning Katie woke to a cold cabin and the sound of loud snoring. She had to go to the bathroom so bad her stomach hurt. Peeking down to the room below, she saw the men passed out on the floor. Katie couldn't wait any longer. She got up and fearfully crept down the ladder, sneaking past her Daddy and outside where she squatted in the snow.

She looked around her, wanting to run away to her Momma, but she didn't know where to go. Shaking from the cold, she returned to the cabin and crept back up to the loft where she waited in fear for her captors to wake up.

Chapter Fifteen

True to his promise Jake arrived at the farm at first light. He'd come on horseback, to assist the sheriff in the manhunt. Joy was up and dressed early. She'd been unable to sleep all night, and felt as though she was wired to an electric current. She knew she wouldn't sleep until Katie was safely in her arms once more. She fixed Jake a mug of coffee while they waited for the sheriff. Blanche and Joe came downstairs a few minutes later, also unable to sleep.

Joe looked at Jake. "I guess I owe you an apology," he said, "for not trusting you with my girl. Now here you are ready to help find my granddaughter, and I want to thank ya."

"Save your thanks till we find her," Jake said. "I haven't done anything, yet." He looked out the window. "Looks like the sheriff's here. Time to get goin'."

Joy grabbed her coat and went outside with him. Sheriff Luke had two men with him, Jake's neighbors, Cal Jenkins and Henry Hawkins. All were on horseback. Both Hawkins and Jenkins wore Deputy's badges, and Luke presented a similar one to Jake. "Let's go look at those prints in daylight," he said. They dismounted and headed to the barn, Joy right along with them.

"Look's like two men and the little girl's prints right here, and over here looks like two horses," said Luke.

"Shouldn't be too hard to track 'em in the snow," said Hawkins.

"Okay, here's what I want you to do," Luke said to the men. "Jake and I will head out. You two wait about five minutes, then follow. I don't want them to catch sight of all four of us at once if we should catch up with them. We don't want to trigger anything that would make them hurt Katie. When we get close, Jake and I will spread out, too.

"Jake, you be ready to grab Katie and run off with her if you get the chance. Don't stick around to find out what's happening to the rest of us. Jenkins and Hawkins will be there as backup by then, and it'll be us three against just two of them, looks like. You're all good shots, so we should be in pretty good shape."

Joy gasped. "Shooting? Around Katie? No!"

"Shhh," Jake put his fingers to her lips. "No one is going to shoot if Katie is in the area. Only after we've got her, and if they try to get away."

"I'm going with you," Joy said. "Wait'll I get Buttons saddled up."

The men looked at each other in alarm. "I don't think that would be advisable," said Luke.

"Joy, listen to me," said Jake. "We're gonna be riding hard and fast, and if bullets do start flying, we don't want you in the middle of them. I believe we can get the job done easier if we know you're safe back here."

"But…"

Jake smiled a sad little smile. "I know how badly you want to see Katie, but this isn't the time to go to her. Trust me, when we find them I'll see that she's brought right back to you." He squeezed her hand, and Joy felt he would be true to his word. It seemed crazy since Stan was so unpredictable, but she knew somehow Jake would keep her Katie safe.

"Okay, Jake, but please take care of Katie."

"As if she were my own," he promised.

The trail cut across the fields to the low hills near the Kanasockett River, then led to the riverbank where they ended.

"Shoot," said Luke. "Looks like they decided to lose any trackers right here."

"They couldn't have gone too far last night since it was near dark when they grabbed Katie," said Jake.

They continued upstream, searching along both sides of the river for fresh prints. It wasn't long before they found them. "Over here, Jake," said Luke. "I didn't think they could keep the horses in that icy water long."

"Poor critters." Jake felt pain for the horses submitted to such cruelty.

The trail now led away from the river towards the highway. The trees became sparse, and it wasn't long before they came upon the horses tethered to a lone Locust and shivering in the cold. Tire tracks led on to the road and disappeared.

"Damn, they've got a vehicle," said Luke. "Looks like truck tires."

Jake's disappointment slammed him in the gut. "No telling how far they went in that."

"Well, I guess there's nothing more we can do here," said Luke.

"Just get these horses to warmth and food," said Jake as he untied the two from the tree. They turned back, joining Hawkins and Jenkins down by the river. "No luck. They got away in a truck, and left these poor critters to freeze to death," Jake told them in disgust.

"We'll have to catch him when he tries to get money from Joy this afternoon," said Luke. They rode back in silence, each man there enraged at the cruelty of the men who'd taken Katie and left two horses to surely freeze to death.

Joy came running out to meet them, but stopped when she saw Katie was not there. She keeled over, clutching her stomach and let out a heartbreaking howl. "My Katieeee!"

Jake felt like his gut'd been split in two. What good were all his promises if he couldn't come up with Katie? He didn't deserve to have Joy's trust if he didn't make good on his promises. "I'm sorry," he said. "The trail ran out. They got away in a truck."

"We're not giving up, Joy," said Luke. "I'm going to raise the money from the bank. Call it a loan. We'll use it as bait. When we catch these guys we'll get it back." He turned to Hawkins and Jenkins. "Now I want you two to come back to town with me and we'll plan how we're going to do this." He picked up his horses' reins.

"Jake, will you keep these two horses we found? Over at your place till we can find out who they belong to? They're most likely stolen from one of the farmers around here. When you get them settled down, come on into town and bring Joy with you."

Joy watched the sheriff and his men leave. She was distraught with worry, but as she turned back to the house her anger at Stan took over. She was not going to let him get away with this.

"Jake, we've got to think, where could he have gone?"

"I dunno, but I wouldn't have thought he'd go very far, since it was already dark, and besides, he's got to come all the way back again today. Can you think of anywhere he might have a hiding place around here? Maybe some place he might have mentioned when you were with him?"

"Noooo."

"What about some friend's place, someone from his past?"

Her forehead wrinkled. "No. Wait, there's his old house where he used to live. But someone else lives there now. And his uncle has a ranch the other side of Pennywhistle. Still, I don't think he'd go there. They never did get along."

"Wal, keep thinkin' on it. Maybe you'll come up with something. I'd best get these horses to my barn, and give 'em some food and a rub down. I'll be back soon's I'm finished."

They gathered in the sheriff's office. Joy sipped on a cup of lukewarm coffee and listened to the sheriff spell out his plan.

"We don't know if they'll have Katie with them, or if Stan'll wait till he gets the money to let you know where she is. So we're going to play this straight. You'll take the money, Joy, and leave it in the tree, then get back to where Jake is. Move fast, but not too fast. I don't want anyone getting suspicious if they're there looking on."

"What if Stan is there when I get to the tree?"

"Same thing. Play it straight. Give him the money and get out quick." He stood up. "Well, I guess it's time we mosey on over there."

"We'll stake out the area first, Jake. Give us fifteen minutes head start, then you and Joy follow. There's an abandoned road from when old Granny Smith used to live in a shack near the river. It's about a quarter mile this side of where we parked to see the tree last night. If you leave your car there it can't be seen from the highway. I'll meet you there and get you two in position."

Katie had to sneak out twice to go potty. Then she crept back to the loft and huddled under the blanket. It was one o'clock in the afternoon before the men stirred. Stan woke up with a pounding headache. To make matters worse the fire had gone out, and there wasn't any dry wood. "Hank, get your butt up and see if you can find some kindlin' around here," he snarled. "So's we can make some breakfast. For Chrissake, I need a G.D. cup of coffee."

Hank rolled over and groaned. "Christ, it's a pneumonia hole in here. Hell, I ain't goin' out in that cold. All the wood out there's wet anyhow."

"I don't care where ya find it, but we need some firewood real quick. I'm goin' to take a pee and I'll hunt up some wood myself while I'm outside. See if you can find somethin' around here for kindlin', will ya?"

"Awright, awright. We can just burn up the wood box. Not likely we'll be usin' this old shack again." Hank smiled a toothy grin, as Katie peered fearfully down on them. Half his teeth were missing and the others were overlarge, looking to her like fangs on a vicious monster. He began tearing apart the slats from the wood box with his bare hands.

Stan returned ten minutes later with a couple of logs he'd found sticking out from under the shack. Hank had forgotten the stash he'd put there a number of years past. Between blowing on the flames and cursing, they managed finally to get the fire to take hold. The damp wood hissed and smoked before at last giving off some heat.

Stan threw some eggs into a pan and scrambled them over the flames, while Hank fixed a pan of coffee. When done, they dumped most of the eggs in two chipped bowls and scarfed them down with stale bread.

Katie was so hungry smelling the eggs cooking that her stomach hurt. But she stayed quiet, not wanting to draw their attention. They were almost finshed before Stan thought of her. "Chrissake, I've got to feed the kid somethin'." He dumped the leftover eggs from the pan into a bowl and shouted. "Katie, get down here."

She descended the ladder and stood before him shaking from the cold and her fear. "Here's your food. Hurry it up," he growled. "We've got a ways to go."

Katie fearfully sat down and took a few bites of the eggs. Hank went outside to bring the truck around, while Stan rolled up their few belongings and kept an eye on her. The little girl shivered. She could barely get the eggs past her chattering teeth.

"Here," Stan said gruffly, throwing an old sweatshirt at her. "Better put this on. You're freezin.'"

She pulled the sweatshirt over her head and almost immediately felt warmer. It fell past her knees, but Katie didn't' care. It was so good to be warm again. "Daddy?" she gathered up her courage to speak. "Why did you bring me here? I miss my Momma."

Stan thought back to the day he'd walked out on Joy. He knew she had tried to get along and be a good wife and mother. He remembered when his own Ma had died. He'd lost her and his little sister within days of each other from the flu epidemic. He'd been about five, not much older than Katie was now, and he'd missed his Ma a lot, too. So much so, that he became very angry, and blamed her for leaving him. It was years before he understood she and his sister hadn't left him by choice. Still, the understanding didn't help him much. He never had trusted women of any age after that. He supposed that was why he couldn't believe Joy would stick by him, so he walked out on her first. Well, that was an old story. He'd made his choices, and he wouldn't get saddled with a family again. "Just get outside to Hank," he told Katie. "It's time to go."

Joy clutched the envelope with the five hundred dollars. The men were in their places hiding in the underbrush along the riverbank. They had been there for about ninety minutes and she was sure they were chilled to the bone. Jake had just ducked into a spot nearer to the road. There was no sign of Stan as she walked slowly to the tree. Brushing aside the acorns, she placed the envelope deep into the recess in the Y. She stepped back, looking up and down the river and called softly, "Katie?" The only sound was the chittering of a squirrel watching from a limb far above. She spoke quietly as she passed Jake's hiding place up on the riverbank. "It's done." As planned, she headed for her car, hidden behind a thicket of dense undergrowth.

There was the sound of a motor from the road. Suddenly Stan leaped out of a truck and approached her. She could see another man waiting in the truck.

"I see you're right on time, Joy."

"Where is Katie?"

"Aw, you don't think I'm gonna tell you that before I get the money, do ya?" He ran down to the tree. Joy retraced her steps, pleading with him to release Katie to her.

"You said you'd leave me a note!"

"Well now, I did, didn't I? Guess I'll have to keep my promise. *When* I'm safely out of town. That's when you'll get the note." He laughed and put his hand into the tree. "Glad to see you brought the money, though I can't see why you'd want to pay all this moola for the brat." He grabbed her arm.

"What are you doing? Let go. You've got your money."

"Just insuring my safety in case you brought anyone with you." He dragged her uphill to the truck, then surprised her with a hard shove, knocking her backwards down the bank. He sprang into the vehicle as Hank revved the engine. They sped away, tires spitting loose rocks, Stan laughing his hoarse cackle, which sent chills through the spines of his hearers. Joy tumbled hard, rolling to a stop against a tree. The men came running to help.

"Joy!" Jake scrambled to her side. "Joy, sweetheart! Are you hurt?" He gathered her up in his arms. She sat up in a daze. Her head smarted where she'd banged it on a rock when she went down and a trickle of blood trailed down her temple. Her face was scratched, caught by some nettles as she'd rolled.

Jake hugged her to him, and gently kissed her forehead. "When I get my hands on him…" he said.

"You'll do nothing, Jake," said Sheriff Luke. "You'll let me lock him up and the law take care of him." Reassured that Joy wasn't badly hurt, he left her to the care of Jake, and scuttled up the hill to recover his hidden vehicle and catch up to his deputies who were giving chase.

"Are you hurt, Joy?" Jake asked again.

"I'm okay, I guess," Joy said. "Why didn't you shoot at him?"

"We couldn't get off a good shot without possibly hitting you. He must have figured that." He felt the knot on her head. "Better get you home, and put some ice on that."

Joy stared at him. "No, Jake, we've got to go after him. We've got to find Katie!" She stood up and started for the road, but lost her balance and would have fallen if he hadn't caught her.

"What's the matter?" he asked in alarm.

"Nothing. I'm just a little dizzy that's all." She leaned against him.

He helped her to her car. "I'll take you home."

"No, you've gotta go with the sheriff. I can drive myself. I'm not dizzy any more."

Jake looked at her doubtfully. He was torn between the need to see her safely home, and his anxiety over what Stan would do to Katie once she was of no more use to him. "Go on, Jake. Please! Help him find my Katie. I'll be all right."

"Well, if you're sure you're okay."

"I'm sure."

Jake kissed her quickly on the cheek, and watched while she turned the car around and headed back toward home. He then raced to where his truck was hidden, and with a screech of tires headed in the opposite direction.

Chapter Sixteen

Joy was beside herself. It was almost dark and the sheriff and his men were not back yet. Blanche and Joe tried to keep her spirits up, but they were equally worried. At last, they heard the sound of a truck in the yard. Not waiting to put on their coats, they spilled out on to the porch.

"Katie? Katie?" Joy screamed, running across the yard to Jake, who was getting out of the truck. He looked at her in sorrow, dreading to tell her he didn't have Katie.

"The sheriff and his men lost them," he said, "but we're not giving up, Joy. I came back to tell you what's happening. But Luke and his men are still out there."

"My Katie, my Katie," Joy sobbed.

It tore Jake up to see her tear-streaked face, angry red scratches on her cheek, and a purple bruise on her temple. If Joy looked this bad from just a few minutes with Stan, he wondered how poor little Katie was faring, and vowed he wouldn't rest until he found her. "Joy, we lost their trail just this side of Pennywhistle. Is there any place where he might be staying in that town? Who does he know there?"

"I don't know," she sobbed.

Jake threw his coat over her shoulders and gently led her back to the house. "I want you to think hard, Joy. Anyone he's kept in touch with back here?"

Joy huddled by the stove, her teeth chattering from the cold. "H-he n-never kept in touch with anyone, not even his brother. Said none of 'em was any good. Th-they washed their hands of him when we left town, and he said he'd never depend on 'em for anything."

"Wal, he's with someone. Stan wasn't drivin' that truck when they got away."

Joy thought back to the figure she'd seen sitting in the truck. A bearded man with wild coarse hair. He'd looked briefly right at her and she remembered the chill she'd felt from his watery dark eyes. There was something vaguely familiar about him.

Closing her eyes, she thought back to high school and the boys that hung around Stan. Suddenly she knew! Henry Abrams, a no-account always in trouble. His hair was wild even back then, though he'd not had a beard, just unshaven sparse whiskers. His father had drunk himself to death she'd heard, and Henry had seemed as though he'd follow the same trail. Stan used to mention him once in awhile. Since they both liked to drink, she wasn't surprised they were back together.

"Jake! It's Henry Abrams he's with. No, Hank. They call him Hank."

"Do you know where he lives?"

"No."

"I heard he moved to Pennywhistle after his folks died," said Blanche.

"Didn't they own a little fishing shack around here somewheres?" asked Joe.

"It's near the river on the other side of Pennywhistle," Joy said. "I remember, now. Stan and I stopped there once when we left home to get married." She looked apologetically at her parents.

"That's it!" Jake smacked his hands together and jumped up from the chair he'd been sitting in. "Do you think you can find it, Joy?"

"I'm not sure. I-I think I can get us close, but it's been a long time and I wasn't payin' much attention to where we was goin' that night."

He grabbed his coat from her shoulders. "Get your coat and let's go. I'll bet anything that's where he's holed up. It's too late for him to go anywhere tonight. The next town's too far away, and from the sounds of him I'd say he's probably more interested, right now, in drinking than driving."

Joy snatched her coat off the hook and ran out the door. "Bye Ma, Pa. We're gonna find her and bring her back."

"Joy, be careful," Blanche said.

Joe put his arms around his wife. "Now Blanche. Jake's gonna take good care of her."

Jake grinned at him. "You bet I am."

Joe nodded. They understood each other. "Now before ya run off, tell me where ya left the sheriff. Blanche and I'll ride out there and let 'em know where yer goin' so they can catch up with ya."

Joy peered out of the truck window at the low hills. The land was mostly barren with the exception of some unusual rock formations. She remembered them from when she'd been here last. The highway wound uphill and gradually the small trees and undergrowth by the roadside became thicker, a sure sign they were getting closer to the river. She spotted a dirt road between a large rock and a broken down fence post. "I think we turned in here," she said. "It's a ways up this road."

They drove a short distance in, then Jake pulled the truck behind a clump of bushes and parked. "Better hike in from here," he said. "Don't want to let 'em know we're coming."

Ten minutes later the road ended in a small clearing. The half moon sent down its dim light to illuminate the scene. Straight ahead sat a small shack with torn roof and sagging porch. The smell of burning wood assailed them.

"Someone's here, all right," said Jake. "I'm going closer to see what's happening inside. You wait here till I get back, then we'll plan what we're going to do."

Joy nodded. She shivered in the cold, while she watched Jake dart as silently as an Indian from tree to tree, until she lost sight of him in the darkness. A moment later she caught sight of his head rising from the porch floor to peek in a window. A torn shade hung crookedly three-quarters of the way down, and Jake peered in through the crack of light at the bottom. She was shaking from her fears and the frigid air when he returned about fifteen minutes later. "Did you see Katie?" she whispered.

"No, but Stan and that Hank character are in there. I'll bet you she's there with 'em."

"What are they doing?"

"They're drinking themselves under the table, looks like."

"What are we going to do?"

"Nothing."

"What do you mean, nothing?" Joy was indignant. "I want my Katie!"

"Joy, listen. They're both drunk. It's only a matter of time before they pass out. I say we just wait and watch, until they're done for. Once they're asleep, there'll be much less chance of anyone getting hurt, even if they do wake up when we go in there." He drew her into his arms and rubbed her back to warm her up. "Now what do you say? Are you willing to do it my way?"

She nodded and hugged him, feeling his strength and warmth. Somehow, she felt, she could spend the rest of her life feeling safe if she were with this man.

Suddenly they heard a noise as the kitchen door opened. "Shhh," said Jake, laying his finger on his lips. They stealthily drew back into the bushes.

Stan lurched outside and hollered. "Hurry it up, Katie. Chrissake, it's damn cold out here. Hell," he muttered, "guess I'll take a pee too, while I'm waitin'." Katie emerged and scurried to a bush where she squatted.

"Oh, Katie!" Joy started to call, but Jake clamped his hand firmly over her mouth, just in time to prevent her drawing attention to their presence.

"Don't, Joy. Not yet. We'll get them, remember our plan?" When she nodded, he released her. "Good." As they continued to watch they saw Stan shove Katie back into the shack with a curse. When she cried out it was all Joy could do to keep from running in and scratching his eyes out, but Jake's arms gently restrained her.

About every quarter hour, Jake returned to the porch to observe the men inside the cabin. "They've killed a six-pack of beer and two fifths of whiskey," he said a half-hour later. They can't even understand each other, their speech is so thick. Shouldn't be long, now." The next time he came back to her, he said, "This is it, Joy. They're fallen down drunk. Passed out on the floor by the stove. Now here's what I want you to do. We'll sneak in there, and I'll hold my gun on 'em while you see if you can find Katie. It looks like there's a back room. She's probably in there. Tell her to be real quiet while we sneak her away. When you get her outside I want you to run as fast as you can for my truck. Then take her straight home. I'll wait here for the sheriff."

She shook her head in alarm. "You can't stay here by yourself. Stan is crazy when he's drinkin'. And there's two of them!"

"Joy, trust me, I'm not going to let them get the upper hand. They won't even know I'm here. Now let's get on inside. Promise me you'll take Katie home."

Reluctantly Joy nodded. Silently they approached the house. As they stepped on to the porch, a slat creaked and Joy froze. Jake by this time was at the window and after checking the occupants he nodded at her reassuringly. He slowly opened the door and they crept inside.

Joy spotted the door to the back room, and headed directly there while Jake stood between her and the men, his gun trained on the two. She wanted to call out to Katie, but bit her lips tight and searched the bedroom. There was a sagging mattress on the floor, heaped high with clothing and a couple of ragged blankets. The room smelled of sour sweat and rotting fruit. There was no sign of Katie anywhere.

She returned to the main room, and shook her head at Jake, who indicated the loft overhead. Furtively she climbed the ladder, and with a muffled cry gathered a sleeping Katie into her arms. Katie squirmed and opened her eyes. "Momma..." she started to say, but Joy covered her mouth with her hands and whispered softly.

"Shhh...Don't make a sound, Katie. We've got to get you out of here. Quickly, now. I want you to go down the ladder and outside without sayin' a word." With a hug, she set her down.

The little girl nodded, her eyes round with fear. When they reached the main room, Katie looked over toward the stove where Stan and Hank flopped on the floor, snoring loudly. "Mr. Jake," she said happily when she spotted Jake standing over them. Joy grabbed her hand and pulled her out the door. It was the snores that saved them, for the kidnappers were making so much noise that they drowned out her voice.

"Shhh," Joy whispered. "Not another word, baby, until we're safe." They ran past the bushes and trees and on up the road to the truck. Joy didn't want to leave Jake behind, but knew she had to get Katie away. Jake had given her his keys, and she started up the engine praying the noise wouldn't wake Stan and Hank. She drove back to the main road and down the highway toward home, Katie sitting quietly and still fearful beside her. It wasn't long before she saw two police cars coming toward her. They passed by, but suddenly turned around and pulled up beside her, indicating she should pull over. It was Luke and his men. "You've got Katie!" Luke said, relieved the little girl was safe. "Where are the others?"

"Oh, thank God you're here, Sheriff. Jake's at the cabin holding a gun over Stan and Hank. They're passed out from drinkin', but I'm so worried they'll wake up and get him."

"Can you tell us just where the shack is, Joy?" Luke asked. "We've got a pretty good idea, but it would help if you give us directions."

"Katie, can you be patient a bit longer while we go back and get Mr. Jake?" asked Joy. "Sheriff, I'll take you there. It's easier than trying to tell you how to find it." She turned the truck around and headed back. When they arrived at the road to the shack, she drove in slowly and pulled over to where she and Jake had been parked earlier. Indicating to the sheriff's men they should go on ahead, she sat in the car and hugged Katie to her.

"Momma, I want to go home," Katie whispered.

"We're goin' home, baby, just as soon as we know Mr. Jake is all right. We'll just wait here for a bit."

Inside the hut, Jake shifted position, wondering how long he could hold out. He wanted to tie up the two men while they were asleep, but didn't want to set his gun down. No telling what they'd do if one of them should wake while he was binding up the other one. Tired of standing, he sank down on to a wooden chair just inside the front door where he could keep them in his sights. He wondered if Katie and Joy were home by now, and breathed a prayer of thanks that they had got to the child before Stan had spirited her away or left her abandoned somewhere.

There was the sound of a board creaking and Jake stiffened, wondering if Stan had another accomplice. He stealthily took up a position behind the door as it began to slowly open. A voice whispered, "Jake," and he knew it was all over. Sheriff Luke and his posse had arrived.

"Glad you're here, Luke." Jake stepped out from his hiding place and greeted the sheriff while Henry and Cal quickly handcuffed the two sleeping men.

"Did you pass Joy on your way?"

"As a matter of fact she led us back here. She's waiting for you outside."

Jake raced to the truck and jumped into the driver's seat, as Joy and Katie slid over to make room for him. "Mr. Jake!" Katie buried her face in his midsection and hugged him fiercely.

"Hi pardner," he grinned at her. "It's all over, honey." Reaching across her, he squeezed Joy's shoulder. "Let's go home," he said.

Blanche ran down the steps when she heard Jake's truck pull into the yard. "Katie, child," she squealed when the little girl hopped down and ran to her, giving her a fierce hug.

"Oh Grammy, I'm back! And I'm so hungry."

"Come in, child. We're all goin' to have some hot stew and fresh bread and butter."

Joe stood on the porch, his arms open wide as Katie ran up the steps. "It's so good to have you back, Katie girl," he mumbled into her neck as he grasped her tightly.

"Grampa! Momma and Mr. Jake found me!" Katie clung to him and looked up in wonder as she saw his wet cheeks. Joe pulled slowly back from the hug. Wiping his tears on his sleeve, he turned to greet Jake and Joy.

"Come in, come in," he mumbled, embarrassed by his tears. "You've found our little girl," he said, embracing them both at once. "Jake, you'll stay and eat with us."

"Don't mind if I do," said Jake. "It smells mighty good."

Katie chattered all during the meal, telling of her experiences. "Daddy took me from the barn. He hit me hard when I said I didn't want to go."

"Did your Daddy hurt you?" Joe was livid, wanting to somehow punish Stan himself. "If he did, I'll…"

"Now Joe," Blanche said. "Don't get yourself all riled up. He's caught now. The sheriff will see that he's put away where he won't do any more harm."

"Daddy said I had to be quiet," Katie went on. "He and that other man drank stuff all the time and used bad words. They made me stay up in the loft and it was so cold."

"Katie, let's get you up to bed," said Joy. "You've had a scare, but it's all over and you're safe now. You'll feel lots better tomorrow, after you sleep."

"I'll go up with her, Joy," said Blanche, needing to keep her granddaughter close.

Jake rose. "That was mighty tasty stew," he said. "I'd best get on over to my own place and let you folks all get some rest. Walk out with me, Joy?"

He held her hand as they walked down to the foot of the steps. Joy smiled up at him, liking the strength of his jaw, caught by the light from the window. "Jake, I can never repay you for helping me get Katie back." Her eyes shimmered with tears threatening to spill over.

Jake pulled her to him. He took out a handkerchief and gently wiped her cheeks just as the first drops fell. "Joy, you were very brave. I didn't do this all by myself you know. We're a team."

"What do you mean?'

"Don't you see? You trusted me. You came to me first when Katic was missing."

"Ye-es."

"Then you trusted me even when I came back without Katie. You trusted enough to follow my plan at the shack even though you wanted to rush right in to her. And the plan worked because we were a team."

She looked up at him in wonder. "Yes we were, weren't we?" she said as she realized how much a part of her he had already become.

He bent toward her and nibbled on her lower lip as he murmured, "We make a great team, Joy. Would you be willing to make it permanent, be my wife?"

Without hesitation, she pulled him closer and murmured "yes." He claimed her lips, nearly devouring her with his kiss, and she felt as though her body were on fire. She snuggled into his sudden, fierce embrace, her kisses equally passionate as she claimed him for her own.

"At last I've come home," she whispered.

Epilogue

Katie was excited. She peered into the mirror as her Grammy pinned her curls up on top of her head. Today her Momma and Mr. Jake were going to get married. They'd built a beautiful log house over by the river near Pennywhistle. She was going to live there with them after a two-week period of time the grownups called a honeymoon, when she would stay here with her grandparents. She didn't understand what a honeymoon was. Her Momma said that was a time for her and Mr. Jake to get to know each other.

"I think they already know each other," she'd said to her Grammy. "Else why would they get married?"

"Hush now," her Grammy had said.

She'd miss living with her Grammy and Grampa, but she could come and stay with them whenever she wanted. And she was looking forward to having her very own friend. A little girl just her age was moving in to Mr. Jake's old house. Her Momma said it was some people who she knew from high school that were the little girl's parents and they were going to be neighbors.

Katie felt very lucky. She had a Grammy and Grampa who loved her, two kittens that she loved, the very best Momma in the whole wide world, and today she was getting a new Daddy who was kind and good to her.

She was to be a flower girl and carry a flower basket for her Momma's wedding, too. Katie grinned at herself in the mirror and twirled her new yellow dress around the room one last time, then ran outside to the yard where the townspeople were gathered for the ceremony.

"Ain't wore a tie since our wedding, Blanche. Can't even remember how to tie the goldern thing," Joe fussed. He shifted from one foot to the other impatiently. "Hurry it up, will ya?" he said as Blanche tried to tie it for him. "Can't be late. I've got to give the bride away, ya know."

"Stand still for a minute, so I can get it tied, Joe. Anyone would think you were the groom instead of the father of the bride." She gave the tie a final pull. "There." She pulled him over to the dresser mirror.

"You look mighty fine, just like when we was married. See?"

Joe, however, caught sight of his wife's pretty pink dress in the mirror, and he remembered their own wedding. She'd worn a white dress trimmed in pink and he remembered how pretty she'd always looked in that color. It was true today as it had been back then. "You should always wear pink, Blanche. You look nice." She blushed and smiled at him. When had Joe last complimented her?

"Are you ready, Joe?" He took her arm.

"I'm ready, Blanche."

They walked down the stairs together. He stood on the edge of the crowd, and spotted his daughter, his soon-to-be son, and his granddaughter.

"It seems we've all come home," he said, pulling Blanche close.

* *